CLARA'S SOLDIER

A RETELLING OF THE NUTCRACKER

BRITTANY FICHTER

ISBN: 978-1-949710-00-7

CLARA'S SOLDER: A RETELLING OF THE NUTCRACKER / Brittany Fichter

Cover Art by Sanja Gombar / https://bookcoverforyou.com/

Edited by Kimberly Kessler

~

And to my sister, Nicole

I'm so incredibly proud of you. Graduating as an Air Force officer is no small feat. And yet, despite your crazy life, you still do your best to care for your "siblings" all over the country. There's something amazing that just can't be put into words when it comes to having best friends from childhood. I'm so thankful to have you.

"...the companions of our childhood always possess a certain power over our minds which hardly any later friend can obtain."
-Mary Shelley, *Frankenstein*

WANT MORE FROM YOUR STORIES?

Sign up for free short stories, exclusive chapters, a no-spam newsletter, and sneak peeks at books before they're published.

Details at the end of this book.

1

LUCKY

*T*he blue gem in Clara's ring glistened in the late afternoon light as she unloaded the crate of cans beside her, its sparkle drawing her attention to the can she held.

Peaches.

Mr. Peters walked in. "What are you smiling at over there?"

"Oh, just these." Clara held up the can then resumed her unloading. "James hates peaches from a can. He says they're slimy." What she neglected to add was that James had once liked canned peaches. Of course, that was before she dared him to eat five jars of them in under ten minutes. He'd won the bet and her nickel, but he never volunteered to eat a canned peach again.

Mr. Peters stepped behind the cash register and took out a paper with a list of figures on it. "Well, I hope he learned to like them."

"Why is that?"

He looked at her over his glasses. "Because during the war, I think Fort Bragg got more canned peaches than the rest of North Carolina combined." He put down his list, his bushy brows furrowed. "Speaking of which, have you heard—"

"No." She forced a too-bright smile. "But when I do, you'll be the first to know." Then before he could ask anything else, she stood and wiped her hands on her apron. "Where's that last crate?"

He pointed, and she went to retrieve it. After dragging the crate to the front of the store, she began again to add to her pile.

As she worked, Clara glanced at her employer. He was still thinking of ways to locate James, judging by his thoughtful frown. The same kind of thoughts, most likely, that had nearly driven Clara insane for the last year. She had to distract him. "When do you think the rations will be over?" She carefully topped off her pyramid of cans.

He tapped his pencil against his mouth. "Don't know. War's been done for over three months now. Should be any time." He glanced around the store and nodded. "But it sure looks much better with its shelves full."

Clara nodded and stood up to survey her work. The store did look pristine. Not an apple, sardine can, or bag of flour was out of place. The boughs of evergreens she'd brought in the day before and wrapped around the door and counters still smelled fresh, and she'd swept up all their fallen pine needles an hour ago. As she was about to move on to inventory, however, she spotted dust on a shelf and bent to wipe it, bumping her head on a higher shelf in the process.

"Ow!" She gritted her teeth and rubbed her head. But feeling sorry for a bump on the head seemed selfish. Especially considering the kind of pain James must have gone through in basic training and then during the war. A headache from a little bump wouldn't worry an American GI on the battlefield. Did the army even give aspirin to its men? Not that he would ask for one. Did he have access to aspirin now, wherever he was?

Before her thoughts could wander too far into dangerous territory, the jingle of the bell above the door interrupted her musings.

A short, plump woman bustled into the shop. She closed the door with a shiver. "Clara, what are you still doing here? I thought Mr. Peters would have sent you home hours ago!"

"I tried," Mr. Peters called from behind the register. "The girl won't leave."

"Happy Christmas Eve, Mrs. Black." Clara grinned. "What can I get for you?" Even as she spoke, however, she began gathering ingredients from the shelves behind her. They'd had this conversation every Christmas Eve since she began working at the grocer three years before.

"Oh, the same as always." Mrs. Black made a face. "I burned the pie again. Told my oldest to watch it for me while I broke up a fight between the two youngest, and by the time I got back, the entire house smelled like smoke."

Clara smiled as she placed the ingredients in Mrs. Black's bag. "Well, at least most of these aren't in short supply anymore. Do you have your ration book?"

"Don't bother with the sugar. My daughter got an earful for allowing the whole pie to go to waste, but I have a little tucked away that the children don't know about yet." Mrs. Black gave Clara a wink. "Saved it just for Christmas. But again, why are you still here?" She peered over Clara's shoulder and scowled. "What trouble are you really up to, Mr. Peters, keeping the girl on Christmas Eve? Tell the truth."

"I told you, Opal." Mr. Peters scowled back. "She won't leave. Spends all her days here cleaning and stocking like a madwoman."

"Have you ever seen someone so busy?" Mrs. Black slipped Clara a small tip with a wink. "I wish my oldest ones would work the way she does." She made a face at the old grocer. "Now, where are those peanuts I asked for last week, you lazy man?"

Clara smiled and picked up the dusting cloth again while the two old friends worked through their typical squabbles.

Her mother had begged her not to go in to work on Christmas Eve, but as the day neared its end, Clara was glad she had. The full shelves gave her a sense of accomplishment. Well, not completely stocked, especially when it came to sugar, but fuller than they'd been in a long time. With the war over, food and other supplies were beginning to roll back into production, even for their tiny North Carolina coastal town.

The shop was not a large one. Old Mr. Peters and his wife never kept or even wanted a large store. Just the one room. Still, it was plentiful enough with floor to ceiling shelves packed with bags of dry ingredients, such as flour, salt, cans of beans, peaches, pepper, and a few boxes of neatly lined fruit and vegetables out front. And now that the war was done and their soldiers no longer needed all their rationed goods, they were once again able to stock coveted items such as nylons, canned milk, and shortening. Candy and sugar were still in short supply, but somehow, Mr. Peters had managed to find enough peppermint sticks to fill the clear glass jar on the counter. Mrs. Peters joked that he was going to run them into debt by giving them all away, though she was no less guilty when it came to sneaking small children a stick or two when their parents weren't looking. But the colors were what Clara liked best. During the war, the brown, bare shelves had seemed dull and lifeless. Filled with food and other goods, as they were now, a promise of better times hung in the air.

And she needed all the promise she could get.

The bell above the door rang again, jarring Clara from her thoughts and interrupting Mr. Peters and Mrs. Black.

"I don't care what they say, Suzanne." A tall woman spoke to the little woman beside her as they walked in. "The doctor calls it shell shock, but I say it's just laziness."

"But he was never lazy before," Suzanne said with a slight frown, breathing heavily as though she'd struggled to keep up with Mrs. McCarty's long strides. "Why do you think he is now?"

"He just got too used to the army taking care of him, that's all." The tall woman rested her basket on the counter beside Clara and ignored the stares of everyone else in the shop.

"I'm going to load some crates up in the back," Mr. Peters called, already out the door.

All on her own, thanks to Mr. Peters, Clara gave the tall woman her best wooden smile as she took her list. "Is your husband well, Mrs. McCarty?" If only she'd beat Mr. Peters to the stock room, then *he* would be stuck with the insipid customer. He owed her for this.

Mrs. McCarty scoffed and tossed her thick black hair. "All that's wrong with my husband is that he needs to get his head out of the clouds and remember what it's like to do some real work. I can hardly get him to mow the lawn, let alone fix the broken window upstairs or trap the mouse that keeps getting into my drawers." She glanced down at the slip of paper in Clara's hands. "Are you going to get that or not?"

Clara looked down at the list. She'd nearly put her thumb through the paper, she was clutching it so tightly. So she pulled herself away from the counter and began piling supplies into Mrs. McCarty's basket. The faster she finished, the faster the awful woman would leave. Hopefully.

"Shell shock is real, you know," Clara said as she worked. She willed her voice to remain calm as she went to the register and added up the total. "The nurses I volunteer with say the men are different after they come home. They—"

"Only want the diagnosis so they can charge for more visits." Mrs. McCarty rolled her eyes as she paid and hefted the basket onto her hip. "All I can say, Clara, is that you should consider yourself lucky James never made it home. At least you can move on with your life and start with someone new. It looks like I'll be stuck with my husband now until one of us dies of old age or madness."

"Mrs. McCarty!"

Everyone turned to see a white-haired woman enter through the back door. Clara relaxed slightly as Mrs. Peters came to stand beside her.

Mrs. Peters ignored everyone else and frowned at Mrs. McCarty. "That is quite enough."

"What?" Mrs. McCarty shrugged. "I'm only looking on the bright side of things."

"Telling a girl it's lucky her fiancé disappeared in the war is hardly looking at the bright side of things," Mrs. Black snapped.

"Say what you want." Mrs. McCarty huffed and turned toward the door. "But the man I married is not the one I'm living with now. I wish it were different, but that's the truth."

Clara's jaw fell open, but Mrs. McCarty either didn't see or didn't care as she stalked out, her friend right on her heels.

Silence filled the shop as Clara walked to one of the windows and examined the glass. If only fingerprints would magically appear so she'd have an excuse to stay on the opposite side of the room, away from the others. She didn't have to look behind her to know that Mrs. Black and Mrs. Peters were watching her.

"I... um. I think the children will be wondering where I am by now," Mrs. Black said after a long moment. She bid them both goodbye and scurried out the door with her groceries as fast as her short legs would take her.

"I know why you work so much."

Clara turned to see Mrs. Peters's sad smile. "I beg your pardon?" She did her best to sound chipper.

"You never stop." Mrs. Peters picked up a rag and wiped the

counter. "You volunteer at the hospital on all your days off. You collected scrap metal for the entire duration of the war." She glanced up at Clara and smiled knowingly. "I did the same thing when my husband was gone during the first war. Threw myself into the store, our children, and the church. If you can name it, I was there."

Clara traced a crack in the glass. "It helps me not to think about him," she whispered. Or, to think about what might have happened to him. Reminiscing was fine, even welcome. But thinking about all the ways he could have been killed or captured or whatever it took to make an American soldier disappear from the face of the planet was a quick path to losing her sanity.

"I know," Mrs. Peters said gently. She laid a warm hand on Clara's arm. "But don't forget that he's not the only one who needs you. Right now, you have a family to get home to." She smiled. "It's Christmas Eve, and you've worked hard enough today. Go home and see if you can help your mother."

Clara hesitated. She should assure Mrs. Peters she was fine and didn't need to go home. Then she could throw herself back into her work with a vengeance. But the lump in her throat prevented her from speaking. So she nodded, took off her apron, and slung her bag over her shoulder. Mrs. Peters's gaze followed her as she left the shop and went around the back for her bicycle.

The day was crisp but not uncomfortable as she rode down the street and across the railroad tracks. Traffic was unusually quiet, even for their small town, as most of the shops, bakeries, and even the gas station were closed. The peaceful streets gave her space to think. Or rather, to avoid thinking and having to report her thoughts to every bystander who looked her way. She was saved from having to answer the question that seemed eternally on everyone's lips, and she was saved from having to restrain herself from retorting that they already knew the answer. If Sergeant James Matthew Parker had come home, everyone would have known it within an hour of his arrival.

They meant well. Everyone, Mrs. McCarty excluded, wanted James to come home. But he wasn't home, and every reminder of that was like a slap in the face.

She meant to head for her house, but instead, she approached the red brick building just off of the main street. Then she parked her bicycle next to the faded blue sign that read, Cape Fear Presbyterian Hospital, and went inside.

Even the building seemed to know Christmas had arrived. The usual smell of rubbing alcohol was somewhat dulled by the faint whiff of ginger, and someone had brought in a scraggly little tree and placed it in the lobby.

"There you are, Clara." A woman with short red curls popped up from behind the front counter. "I was wondering if you were going to come in today." She held up a plate of gingerbread cookies. "Want one? One of the mothers brought them in this morning."

Clara did her best to smile. "Hi, Sue. No thanks. I'm on my way home. This is just a quick stop."

"Aw, no reading today? The kids have been asking when you'll be back."

Clara played with a stray lock of hair. "I'll be back next Tuesday. Things have just been...."

"I know, hun. You don't have to explain."

Clara cleared her throat. "I just thought I would stop in and ask—"

But Sue was already shaking her head. "You would be the first person to know, believe me." She glanced down at a stack of papers on the desk. "I promise, I'm watching for any sign of him." She shrugged and gave Clara a sad smile. "Most of the soldiers are home by now. Or at least accounted for. I haven't been getting many new patients for the last couple of weeks. At least, not out of the ordinary."

Clara nodded and began to turn away, but before she could leave, Sue reached out and grabbed her wrist.

"You know what? I've got a friend who just started working up north at Walter Reed, that naval hospital in Maryland. I'll give her a call and tell her to keep her eyes open."

Clara squeezed her friend's hand. "Thanks, Sue."

Sue's eyes softened. "If you don't give up on him, neither will we. Now, I want you to go home and have a merry Christmas Eve with your family. None of this despair business. And next Tuesday, I expect to see you back here with a book in hand, ready to read to those children." She quirked an eye. "Deal?"

Clara laughed. "Deal."

"And I'll make that call, I promise." Sue was already scribbling on a pad of paper. "Now go enjoy your Christmas Eve party before I drag you home myself."

Clara shrugged off her disappointment as she made her way back to her bicycle. Sue was right. She would have called the moment she'd heard something about James. And yet, Clara had hoped....

"Mr. Peters said I might find you here."

Clara looked up to see a burly young man park his bicycle next to hers.

"Hi, Edward." She smiled, and for once, it wasn't forced.

He nodded up at the hospital. "You reading to the kids today?"

"No, but I will be next week." She turned her bicycle and began to walk it toward the road. "Do you read to them?"

"Nah." He picked his bicycle up again and followed her. "Sue tried to rope me into it once, but you know I read like a third grader. Besides, you're a whole lot prettier to look at."

"I started back after James quit writing." She stopped walking, and her throat tightened. "I wanted to feel useful."

Edward rubbed the back of his neck and looked at the sky. "I know what you mean." Then he chewed on his lip. "Hey, you got a minute?"

"Sure."

He hopped on his bike, and she followed suit, letting him take the lead.

2

ONE OF US

Clara followed Edward down the road. The sun was descending in the afternoon sky, and the air was decidedly chillier by the time they stopped at the edge of an old baseball field. Without a word, Edward hopped off his bike and laid it on the ground before climbing onto the faded wooden fence that surrounded the sandy field.

Clara climbed up beside him. He pulled a handful of sunflower seeds from his pocket and held them out. She took some and sorted them by size in her hand.

"So," she said, "why did you need to find me?"

Edward's easy expression disappeared, and his dark brows knit together. "I heard what Mrs. McCarty said."

She rolled her eyes. "I should have known everyone would have heard by now."

"Eagle Head might be some mediocre North Carolina town, but we could beat out the telegraph with our gossip chain." Edward shook his head as he spit out a shell. "Mrs. Black told my neighbor who told my mother." He paused and looked at Clara. "Wait… would you rather be alone right now? If you don't want to talk to me, I can leave."

She gave him a reluctant smile and shook her head. "You know I'm always glad to see you. And thanks for coming." She looked down at the seeds in her hand and sighed. "It's the town and all their pity that I can't stand."

"They're just trying to be nice."

"I know." She cracked a seed with her teeth and spit it out. "But they don't just act like he's dead or missing. Most of them seem afraid to admit he ever existed. They won't even say his name. Even his parents. The last time I went to their house, his baby picture was off the wall." Edward was watching her, but she avoided his eyes and stared out at the field. "At least..." She swallowed hard. "At least you and Sue and Mr. Peters acknowledge that he's somewhere." Her heart clenched, and she squeezed the seeds in her hand until she felt several pop.

"I miss him, too."

She looked up.

Edward wiped at the corners of his eyes. "He was my best friend first, you know." He chuckled and bumped his shoulder against hers. "Before you came and stole him away." Then he sucked a deep breath in through his nose. "I can't help wondering if it weren't for this stupid knee, they might not have turned me away at the recruiter's, and I might have been there with him, and he never would have—"

"You can't think like that, Edward," she said softly. "God kept you here for a reason." She sat up straighter and tried to laugh. "Who else would the girls look at with all the other boys away?"

Edward gave her a funny look. "So you think I'm handsome?" His voice was teasing, but there was something in his eyes that was a little too serious for her taste.

She slid off the fence and leaned back against it with her arms crossed. "Well, you know, compared to Iggy. And he's the next best thing."

Edward snorted. "Great. That makes me feel much better. At least I'm more attractive than my best friend's dog."

She burst out laughing, and he joined her. Eventually, though, they grew quiet. A breeze whipped around them, and Clara pulled her coat tighter. The field was empty now, all except for them. But even without laughing, shouting children surrounding them, the memories flooded back the same way they always did. If she closed her eyes and listened to the wind, his voice might come floating in on it. Even when he was teasing, his voice was warm and rich, like hot chocolate.

Unlike all the other boys their age, James's voice had skipped right through the awkwardness of puberty. One day, when they were twelve, he said goodbye to her like he always had. The next morning, he'd greeted her with the voice of a young man. She'd picked a fight with him that afternoon just so she could hear more if it.

"By the way," Edward's voice interrupted her musings. "I know exactly what you did that day."

"What day, and what exactly did I do?"

Edward elbowed her. "The day you hit James with a baseball? I know you did it on purpose."

"Why, Edward Joseph Hendricks!" She whirled around to whack him in the shin. "Take that back!"

"You did, too! I saw you!" He pointed at the dusty home plate. "You were the pitcher. He was up to bat, but he was making eyes at Cathy instead of paying attention to you. And I saw you look back and forth between them twice." He held up two fingers as if to prove his point. "Then you beamed him in the head with the ball."

"Can't a girl miss sometimes? Even the great Ted Lyons misses now and then." Clara tried to keep the smile off her face at the memory. But she couldn't.

"Nah, you looked right at him and gave him that little evil

grin, the same one you're wearing now. You didn't even look at his bat." Edward pursed his lips and shook his head. "Eleven years old, and you were cunning enough to know James Parker couldn't resist a girl who threw a baseball like a pro."

"You can't blame me for one bad pitch."

He hopped off the fence and stood beside her. "No, but I can blame you for stealing my best friend. He followed you around like a puppy from then on until the day he shipped out."

For a long time, they stared at home plate. It was a lot dirtier than it had been when they were little, and a big crack ran right down the middle. But it was the same home plate James had stepped on a thousand times. Just like this whole town, it reeked of memories with no end, like interrupted songs.

"I need to get going." She climbed down the fence and headed to her bike.

"Yeah, me, too." Edward followed her. "I'm looking forward to tonight, by the way. What time is it again?"

"Seven-thirty. And that makes one of us." Then without waiting to hear his reply, she hopped on her bike and pedaled for home.

3

ALWAYS JAMES

Clara pedaled until sweat rolled down her back and temples. She'd stayed too long at the baseball field, and her mother would be worried. She raced over the railroad tracks, past the library and the church, and over the little bridge into her neighborhood, where she was greeted by rows and rows of white peaked roofs and little picket fences surrounding every yard.

Though the war was over, most of her neighbors still had their victory gardens, and most of them looked better than hers. "Sow the seeds of victory!" the government signs had all said. "Our food is fighting!" And Clara had tried. She really had. She'd sewn her seeds in an effort to grow food for her family so more supplies would be freed up for the war effort. But try as she might, nearly all of her vegetables died before they were a month in the ground. Her mother had eventually set her to gathering the plants rather than tending to them. That part of the war effort Clara did not miss.

She was almost home when a flash of gold caught her eye, and she braked in front of her neighbor's house. A second gold star hung in their window where it hadn't that morning. She closed her eyes and said a prayer for them before moving on to her home. Another son dead. The oldest son had been lost less than a month after setting foot on European soil, and their second and fourth sons had been too injured to travel home, last she heard. Now she prayed a third star wouldn't join the other two. The war was over and had been since September, but some days it seemed like the blood spilled just as much as it ever had during the fighting.

She put her bike in the alley behind her house and went in through the back door. Before she got very far, a hand grasped her wrist and pulled her into the little alcove under the stairs.

She gasped. "Aunt Pearl! I thought you weren't going to be—"

"My boss let us off early. Now come upstairs before your mother realizes you're home and puts you to work." Without waiting for an answer, her aunt dragged her upstairs and into Clara's bedroom.

"Whatever we're doing," Clara whispered as they reached the top of the stairs, "Mother will need my help soon with setting the table and getting the dishes ready."

"Nonsense." Her aunt scrunched up her face. "She may want it, but she doesn't need it. I've done so much baking today even your brother won't be able to eat it all. Now close and lock the door. I've got something for you."

Clara couldn't help smiling as she closed the door behind them. Of all the dozens of relatives that were coming to her family's annual party, her mother's little sister was her favorite. As usual, Aunt Pearl's thick blond hair was piled high up on her head. A few strands might have glinted silver in the light of the setting sun coming through Clara's window, but other than that and a few wrinkles at the corners of her eyes, she looked just as young and trim as ever.

"Here!" Aunt Pearl held out a blue dress. "I was going

through my wardrobe, and as soon as I found this dress, I knew immediately it was meant for you."

Clara took the dress. "This is so sweet. But are you sure? It's so nice."

"Oh, it's nothing but a patched up gown that's too young for me now. Put it on. I want to see."

There was no use arguing with her aunt when she was excited, so Clara did as she was told. She stood in front of the mirror as Aunt Pearl got down on her knees and began to pin.

"And to think," her aunt gushed as she finished stitching the bottom of the skirt, "soon all this rations nonsense will be behind us, and I'll get to take you department store shopping again instead of fixing up my dusty, old gowns. Now, step back and let me look at you. Turn. Yes, that's it. Keep turning."

Clara did as she was instructed. It really was a lovely dress even if it was old and patched up as Aunt Pearl continued to lament. The blue fabric was the same shade as a robin's egg, and the buttons were the color of cream. "It's perfect," Clara said, swishing the skirt from side to side. "The dress looks as good as new."

That didn't stop her aunt from fussing about proper length lines and whether the skirt had the right amount of flair for the modern mode.

Finally, though, she stepped back and sighed. "James would have given the world to see you in this. I'm sure of it." She pulled Clara's long hair back, but after wrestling with her thick, wavy curls for five minutes, gave up and decided to leave it down. "The dress matches your eyes. It also brings out the darker shades in your hair."

Clara twirled a little to see how far the dress would flair out. "This was his favorite color." She turned to her aunt and took Aunt Pearl's hands in hers. "I mean it, thank you."

Her aunt's lips were pinched and her eyes were red as she

made a few last adjustments to the skirt. But they were running out of time. Through the window, they saw guests beginning to arrive, all bundled up against the cold.

Clara took a deep breath. As far as she was from ready, it was time. She put on her shoes, hugged her aunt, and ventured downstairs.

"Well, look at you!" Clara's father greeted her at the bottom of the stairs. His old brown suit, though somewhat worn in places and covered in more patches than she remembered, fit better than it had since she was a little girl. That was probably a testament to the food rations that he, more than anyone else, hoped would end soon.

He caught her hand and twirled her around in a circle. "You look like a Christmas fairy!" Then his smile faded. "I know this'll be difficult for you, Little Bear. If it gets to be too much, just give me a sign, and you'll be excused."

She hugged her father. "Thank you." Then she drew a steadying breath. "People are going to talk. It's what they do. It's probably best if I just get it out of the way and prove to everyone that I'm going to be fine."

Her mother, who had joined them while Clara was speaking, exchanged a worried glance with her father.

"Really, I'll be fine." Clara took her mother's hand and squeezed it. "I'm not the only one missing someone this Christmas." And yet, her eyes moved to the little diamond ring on her left hand.

Before her parents could respond, footsteps thundered down the wooden floor toward them.

"Clara!" Fritz, her little brother, ran into her at top speed, nearly knocking her over. "You should see the table! I've never seen so much food!" He counted on his fingers. "There are apples and oranges and meat pies and pecan pies and chocolate and even coffee!" His brown eyes gleamed as he jumped up and down, his shoes making terrible clunking sounds each time he landed on the hardwood floor.

Clara laughed as she reached down to rub his brown curls and straighten the collar on his shirt. "Careful not to eat yourself into a coma." She winked at him. "Then I might have to open your presents."

"Fritz." Their mother frowned at her son. "You're going to put a hole in the floor. Now, come greet our guests and leave the dining room alone."

"But Mom...." Fritz obeyed, but he protested all the way to the entryway.

Her father chuckled and turned back to her. "You ready?"

She took her father's arm as they walked toward the front room. "Where did we get so much food? Judy told me that the sugar rationing won't end for quite a while."

"Your mother has invited anyone we have even a chance of being related to, and they all shared. Now remind me, what does Judy's father do again?"

"He works in D.C. He wrote to her yesterday to tell her not to get rid of her old shoes. It'll be a while before she'll be able to get new ones."

Her father stopped at the edge of the entryway. Noise was already spilling in from the front door where aunts and uncles, grandparents and cousins, and even a few neighbors greeted her mother and thanked her profusely for the invitation. He rubbed her knuckles between his calloused fingers. "Now, you're sure—"

"Yes, Father." She mustered a grin. "I may not have James, but...." She looked around their home. Garlands that she and Fritz had cut the day before were wound around every post and surface. The aromas of dishes she hadn't tasted in years were wafting in from the dining room, and the air vibrated with an excitement that none of them had felt for a long time. "We have a lot to be grateful for."

"Yes." He kissed the top of her head. "We certainly do."

As soon as they stepped into the entryway, both she and her father were engulfed by relatives. In just moments, she passed through the arms of an uncle, two cousins, and a great-grandmother before she finally found herself in the unfortunate embrace of Aunt Marla.

"Merry Christmas, Aunt Marla." She tried gracefully to dance in and out of the hug, but her aunt was surprisingly strong and had a firm hand on her elbow before she could escape.

"Step back, let me have a look at you," Aunt Marla said.

Clara fought the urge to grimace. It was amazing how Marla and Pearl could say the same exact words, and yet Marla made them sound like an order from the military drill instructor James had written about in one of his letters.

Marla pursed her shiny red lips as Clara obediently turned in a circle. "Well, you haven't wasted away too much. If I'm honest, I'd expected far worse for a girl who lost her fiancé."

A hot flush crept up Clara's neck. A few relatives standing nearby looked uncomfortable as they paused in their joyous reunions and stared at her aunt. Just as Marla looked like she might say something worse, however, a deep, rumbling voice spoke up.

"I hope I'm not interrupting."

Clara turned with great relief to the older gentleman standing behind her. His mat of silver hair was wilder than usual, and his beard less than neatly trimmed. But the steel in his voice and the way his gray eyes darkened as they stared down her aunt made it very clear he had every intention of interrupting.

"Godfather!"

She threw her arms around him, inhaling the scent of black-market tobacco and wood shavings.

As soon as he'd won the staring contest with Marla, her godfather, Nigel Drosselmeyer, wrapped her in a big hug.

She beamed up at him. "You made it!"

"Of course I made it." His thick eyebrows almost touched as he scowled. "When have I ever missed Christmas Eve with you?"

"You've been late nearly every single year."

"Ah." His eyes twinkled, and he reached into his jacket and pulled out a stopwatch. "That's because I keep forgetting to have this old thing tuned."

"You know you are perfectly capable of tuning it yourself. And you live next door." She laughed, though it was still somewhat shaky.

He scoffed. "But I always forget. I'm too busy with important things to worry about inconsequential details such as time." Then he clapped his hands and rubbed them together. "Now, I smell coffee. How about we get your old godfather some rationed goodness and then we find a place to sit?"

She grinned. "I've already set your favorite mug aside."

They filled their plates with decadent treats and sat on the edge of the noisy party. Then they ate in silence until her godfather put down his empty plate and turned to her, an expectant look on his wrinkled face.

"So how are you, really?"

The warmth of his gaze and the simplicity of his question released something in Clara's stomach that she hadn't known was so tightly wound. "I'm alright," she said quietly. She gazed at the merry festivity everyone else seemed to be basking in. "I'm grateful the war is over, but..."

"But you miss him." It wasn't a question, just a statement of fact.

She nodded. "It's not as though I'm not used to missing him, but with the Germans' POW camps being emptied now," she swallowed hard, "I'd hoped." She'd hoped. What a stupid thing to do.

Drosselmeyer simply nodded and placed his hands under his chin.

"What's worse," Clara continued, still watching the merry-making that surrounded them, "is their pity. They watch me out of the corners of their eyes. I can see it. It's like they don't even see me anymore. All they can see is the girl who believed in the fantasy that her hero might come home and that life might one day be normal again." She played with one of the cream-colored buttons Aunt Pearl had sewn onto the front of her dress. "And they're probably right."

"You know," her godfather said, taking her hand in his weathered one, "you used to believe that I could do Christmas magic." He leaned in a little closer, his dark eyes boring into hers. "Are you too old to believe that now?"

She gave him a tired smile. "That was a long time ago, Godfather."

He nudged her shoulder. "I've got a little Christmas magic left. Are you sure you don't want to make a wish?"

She rubbed her eyes and chuckled. "Well, then, if you find no one else to use it on, I suppose you could always try to figure out my wish."

Her godfather scoffed. "Well," he groaned as he rose stiffly to his feet. "You may not believe in such things anymore, but this old man has some non-magic to perform for those who still do. Come and help your godfather get his things. I promised Fritz and his cousins a puppet show before supper."

Clara rose to her feet and slipped her arm in his as they walked toward the door where he'd dropped what she used to call his magic bag.

"I forgot to ask," Clara said. "How was your recent trip up to Raleigh?"

Before he could answer, they were accosted by Fritz and the rest of the younger cousins who begged and pleaded for their promised puppet show.

Even if she hadn't been trying to avoid Aunt Marla, there were few things in the world that Clara liked better than helping her godfather set up his puppets. They weren't really puppets, but figurines he carved from small bits of wood. If she hadn't known better, the lifelike figurines would have tempted her to believe in magic once more. Never, even in the big department stores, had she ever found toys with such lifelike features. From the gentle curves of their cheekbones down to their chins, necks, and even their ears, every inch of the dolls was carved with love.

She had gotten to watch him carve on several occasions as a little girl when her mother wanted to take her shopping and Clara would throw a fit.

"I want to stay with Godfather," she would whine.

"Let her stay with me," Drosselmeyer would cajole her mother. "I always carve a little better when I have inspiration." And he would wink at Clara, knowing they had won the battle. Then she would sit on a little stool in the corner of his workshop and watch as he carved each piece with fastidious care. The first time she watched him, he took nearly an hour to carve a single face. The little figurines that he carved, sanded, and painted stayed locked up in special boxes for most of the year, but each Christmas, they came out to cheer the little boys and girls.

Tonight the grown-ups cleared a table for the little ones, and Clara helped her godfather set up the figurines with the tiny furniture he'd carved for them as well. Before long, he was making the little voices and funny sounds to tell the stories she remembered from her own childhood.

But for the first time in her twenty-one years, Clara couldn't find the same contentment in the show as she always had before. But then, she'd struggled all week with finding contentment in anything.

Usually, she was an expert at staying busy. Whether she was working for the war effort, collecting scrap metal, reading to the children at the hospital, taking care of Fritz, or working for Mr. Peters, Clara kept her mind off, at least in part, of James. And after his letters stopped coming, she'd become even busier, making sure she was too involved in everything to wonder whether he was in a German prisoner of war camp, or whether he was getting enough to eat. She refused to even entertain the idea that he might not be coming home.

But now that the war was over, and the holidays meant an overabundance of grandmothers, aunts, and cousins preparing the family's big feast, she found entirely too much time to think. And with her thoughts came James. Always James.

As her godfather moved the figurines toward the end of his story, the same tale he had told countless Christmases before, Clara wished, for one brief moment, that she still believed in Christmas magic. The kind she'd once believed him to possess.

Applause and cheering interrupted her thoughts.

"I'm afraid I'm getting too old for this." Drosselmeyer plopped down in the chair beside her and laughed.

"Here." She handed him a mug of cider. "You've earned it."

He took the drink with a nod. "Why did your parents and all of their siblings decide to have so many boys all at the same time?" He rubbed his back woefully. "They take ever so much more energy than girls."

She laughed. "I believe there were seven boy cousins born in the same year. And you'll never be too old for this. The show was just as marvelous as ever."

He reached into his pocket and pulled out a small wrapped box, about the length of her hand. Holding it out, he leaned toward her with an ornery grin. "Hopefully, you're not too old for this."

Despite her age, Clara's heart thumped unevenly as she took the box and removed the ribbon. Could it be what she hoped it was? She lifted the lid, and her heart soared. Sure enough, there lay a figurine gazing back at her out of piercing blue eyes. She let out a cry of delight.

"You made one for me?" After pulling the little nutcracker from its box, she gently fingered all the fine details, from the army green jacket with its dark buttons down to the coal black boots and the little silver sword strapped to his side. "He looks just like him," she whispered.

The resemblance to James was uncanny. Their eyes were the same shade of ocean blue, and the chin was barely cleft enough to notice. Though somewhat gangly, the little wooden man's lean build gave off a subtle strength. And while the nutcracker's jaw had been shaped to open and close, a slight upturn to the right corner of his mouth and a twinkle in his eye suggested some sort of mischief.

She turned to gaze at her godfather wistfully. "Are you sure you don't have enough Christmas magic left for something besides wood carving?" She gave a little laugh. "When I look at this, I could believe near anything."

She expected him to chuckle along with her, but instead, his eyes grew mysterious, and with a sad smile, he leaned in just a little. "I'm afraid my magic has almost run dry," he whispered. Then he tapped her nose with his finger. "But for you, my dear Clara, I shall do my best." He seemed about to say something more, but then he looked over her shoulder. "May I help you?"

Edward was standing behind her. He looked fetching in his blue suit, though his pants were about two inches too short. His dark hair was slicked back, and for once, his fingernails were clean.

"Godfather." She stood and gently nudged Edward forward. "This is Edward. He's James's best friend."

Edward raised his eyebrows a little and gave her a funny look. "I've known you a minute, too."

She laughed. "We all went to school together. From first grade all the way up."

"And why are you here, exactly?" Drosselmeyer stood as well. His face was serene as he gestured to the bustling scene around them. "I've been attending the Frosts' Christmas Eve parties since before Clara was born, and I've never seen you before."

She nearly choked on her cider, and Edward stared at the old man as though he'd been asked to walk on hot coals.

"Godfather!" She wasn't sure if she should laugh or scold the old man. So she chose to laugh nervously as she tried to brush the spilled cider off her bodice. Each man offered her his handkerchief. She took them both. "Mother invited him." Really, what had gotten into Drosselmeyer?

Before her godfather could form a response, the little nutcracker was yanked from Clara's hand. She looked over just in time to see Fritz waving it around excitedly.

"It's a soldier!" he shouted at his friends, holding the nutcracker up high. "This is great, Clara!"

But before she could warn him to be careful, Fritz tripped backward over a toy cannon that had been left in the middle of the floor. The nutcracker flew through the air and landed on the ground with a loud crack.

4

AFTER JAMES

Clara ran to where the nutcracker lay and knelt beside it. She lifted it with trembling hands. The nutcracker's jaw had fallen slack, and every time she tried to close it, it fell open again.

Fritz scrambled to his feet beside her, but when he saw the nutcracker, his face went white. "I'm-I'm so sorry, Clara. I didn't mean to. I—"

Clara felt the tears coming. But for some reason, this was one cry she couldn't bite back. So she bore her shame in front of the entire family as she sat there on her knees, clutching the wooden doll to her chest. The practical voice inside her head told her she should get up, dry her face, and find some way to stay busy. But she couldn't even get to her feet. Instead, she simply knelt on the floor and sobbed like a little girl, the broken nutcracker lying limp in her arms.

For an eternal stretch, the only sounds that echoed through the large room were Clara's cries and Fritz's apologies. Then came Aunt Marla.

"Do you see, Jonathan?"

Everyone, including Clara, looked up at her aunt. But Marla

didn't take the hint. Instead, she continued talking at her husband, not noticing how his face was turning a bright shade of red. "This is why I've said all along that she needs to get over that boy." She turned to Clara. "When your mother wrote to me, saying that your fiancé hadn't returned, but that you were holding out hope, I knew you were going to let yourself pine away to nothing." She rolled her eyes and put a chubby hand to her breast. "The makings of an old spinster, if I ever saw one. A young woman in the prime of her youth who won't accept the fact that her loved one has been bludgeoned to death or shot or brought to his early grave in some horrid way by those Nazis—"

"Marla!" Clara's mother cried, but Marla blundered on.

"You know." She fixed Clara with a stern gaze. "It's probably a good thing you didn't get married before he left. It's been what, two, maybe three years?"

"Three," Clara said through gritted teeth. James had been gone for three years. Three Christmases with just a ring and a picture and the few letters he had sent. And one and a half years since the last letter had come.

But Marla wasn't finished. "Just think, if you two had gotten married before he shipped out, you would be an official war widow now. Then forget about getting married again. What man wants used goods like that? And that boy wouldn't have—"

"His name is James."

Marla stopped and stared.

Clara didn't even realize she'd spoken until the words were out of her mouth. But as soon as they were, she realized that she wasn't done. So she cleared her throat and spoke in slow, measured tones. If she wasn't careful, she would end up using words that would make Grandma Hannah faint.

"His name," she whispered, getting to her feet, still clutching her little nutcracker, "is James. He was born in 1924. We attended school together every day of our lives. When we were eleven, I hit him in the head with a baseball, and he says he's loved me ever since." She took a step toward her aunt, her voice growing in volume with every word. "He's wanted to be a soldier since he was five, and as soon as he turned eighteen, he put on this uniform." She thrust the nutcracker in her aunt's face. "And he left to protect people like me and, unfortunately, people like you from the evil that has starved and gassed and tortured millions of people to death." The tears streamed down her face, but her heart beat more fiercely in her chest with each passing second. "And maybe you're right. Maybe I am on my way to becoming an old maid. But people will see that I have loved so deeply that any attempt to replace that would be a stupid waste of time."

Clara's mother came to stand beside her. She took Clara's arms. "Let's go upstairs."

But Clara wasn't ready to leave. And her mother's gentle attempts at pulling her away only invigorated her as she stared into Aunt Marla's indignant eyes. "His name is James, and he was never just *that* boy."

Grandmother Hannah was the first one to break the awkward silence. "I think supper should be nearly done." She made eye contact with the other women in the room. "Let's go get the food on the table, shall we?" The women followed, and the men took their cue and cleared the room as well, leaving Clara's family, Marla, Drosselmeyer, and Edward, who looked like he wanted to melt into the floor.

"Marla, you are my sister," Clara's father said in a low voice. "But if you ever speak to my daughter like that again, you will no longer be welcome in my home."

Clara's mother said nothing, but she tugged on Clara's arm. "Let's go upstairs and wash your face."

Clara shook her head. She refused to be beaten by her bully of an aunt.

Marla sniffed and straightened her skirt, then headed for the kitchen.

Clara watched her go, angry tears still rolling down her face.

Her godfather gently took the nutcracker from her hands and tied his handkerchief around the nutcracker's jaw. "I think," he said softly, "that some soldiers meet their end in battle." His eyes twinkled. "But others simply need a good nurse and a little bit of magic to help them find their way home."

Clara's mother gently urged her up the stairs once more. This time, with one more reassuring glance from her godfather, she acquiesced.

Upstairs, her mother sat her in front of the vanity. Then she left, only to return again with a bowl of warm water. She dipped a warm rag inside and began to wipe away Clara's smeared makeup. The giant grandfather clock in the hall boomed the eighth hour of the evening, time for supper. Her mother, however, didn't hurry to get them back downstairs. Instead, she finished cleaning Clara's face and then began to apply powder to her cheeks once again.

As relieving as the silence was, Clara waited until she could stand it no longer. Her mother's touch, which was usually gentle, was now agitated, her hands moving in quick, short bursts. Clara finally turned to her mother and put her hand up to stop the little brush from dusting her cheeks.

"You think Marla's right, don't you?"

Her mother stared down at the powder, her brows furrowed. "Marla is never right. I've believed that with all my heart since I married your father twenty-five years ago. The way she talked to you just now was inexcusable."

"But?"

Clara's mother sighed and put the powder down. Still, she

did not meet Clara's gaze. "Clara, have you looked in the mirror lately?"

Clara turned back to the mirror. Her chestnut hair, which had been neat and shiny when she'd gone downstairs, was now messy, and strands stuck out all over the place.

Her mother began brushing it.

"What do you mean?" Clara asked. She hadn't gained or lost much weight in several years, and she looked decently healthy, at least from what she could tell.

"You don't see it?" Her mother was frowning now. Then she huffed and shook her head as she twirled Clara's locks in her fingers to pin them up. "It's been a long time since James went missing."

Clara's throat tightened. She took a blue hair ribbon from the vanity and nervously wrapped it around her hand. Now was probably not the time to add that even James's own parents had given up looking for him after last Christmas. "Yes."

"A very long time." Her mother tugged on her hair a little too hard for comfort. "And for over a year, I've had to watch you develop this... this hole. You look like your nutcracker."

Clara swallowed a cheeky reply that green wasn't her color. She would get another lecture for trying to wiggle out of whatever her mother was trying to tell her, which she was growing surer by the minute she would dislike.

Her mother waved a hand and frowned. "You smile enough, and you're always busy. But I miss your spark. The fire in your eyes is gone. It's as if... it's been extinguished."

Because my spark's been working overtime to keep my heart beating, she wanted to reply. Instead, she sat up straighter. "And you wouldn't feel the same way if you lost Father?"

Her mother's hands paused before moving even faster. "That's different. Your father and I are married."

"James and I would have been married."

Clara's mother leaned forward to look straight into her eyes. "But you weren't. And no amount of wishing is going to change that." She scowled and went back to doing Clara's hair. "If James could see you now, do you think he'd be happy? Do you think he would want you to live the rest of your life like there's a hole inside of you?"

Clara's face heated, and she gripped the edge of her chair. "You talk like he's never coming home."

"Clara, I want James home more than anyone." Her mother paused and rubbed her eyes. "Possibly even more than you. Because if he was home, you'd start living again. But thousands of boys never came home. And as much as we all love him, James was not magically immune to the Nazis or the cold and rain or sickness or—"

"Are you finished?" Clara glared at her mother in the mirror.

Her mother put her hands on her face and took a deep breath. When she finally opened her eyes once more, her voice was more controlled, and her brown eyes were no longer burning. "I'm not going to ask you to make a decision tonight. But I need for you to at least come to terms with the fact that the day is near when you'll need to make that choice."

"What choice?"

"You're going to have to choose to move on. One day, you'll have to choose. No one else can do it for you."

The lump in Clara's throat was too big for her to speak, so she stood stiffly and made her way to the door.

Before she could shut the door, though, her mother called out. "Rude or not, Marla had a point. You can't pine for the rest of your life, Clara. James wouldn't have wanted it."

Clara had to work hard not to slam the door shut and stomp down the hall to the stairs. Her heart was beating so fast her head spun. But even there she found no reprieve. At the bottom of the stairs, she found Edward looking up at her as though he'd been waiting. His eyes wore that same funny look they had that afternoon at the baseball field. Clara nearly sighed aloud.

"Go to him," her mother whispered from behind, making Clara jump. "At least hear what the boy has to say."

Clara's first inclination was to do the exact opposite of what her mother suggested and lock herself in her room. But that would not be kind to Edward. After all, it wasn't his fault James was gone.

Edward waited for her to reach the bottom of the stairs, a slight sheen of sweat glistening on his forehead. "Clara, can I talk to you outside?"

He deserved better, but all she could give him was a sharp nod before heading for the back door.

He followed her through the kitchen full of women. The chatter dulled the moment she stepped through the door, and she could already imagine the gossip that would take place the moment they were on the back porch. But she held her head high and pretended she wasn't reeling until they were outside.

The soothing sound of waves on the distant beach greeted her. She shivered in the chilly air and regretted not grabbing her coat. But before she could dart back in to get it, a larger, thicker coat was placed over her shoulders. It smelled of firewood and wheat.

"Thank you," she said stiffly, trying not to act too grateful. It was just a gesture after all. Any gentleman would do the same for a woman. "Think it'll snow tonight?" She went to the porch's ledge and peered up at the now overcast sky.

"North Carolina doesn't usually get snow this time of year, especially not on the coast." His voice was unusually gravelly.

"I hope it snows. A white Christmas would be like my own little miracle."

But for once, Edward stayed quiet. Clara slowly edged

herself into the corner where she could lean against the post and tightly hug her middle.

After several minutes of awkward silence, Edward shoved his hands in his pockets and looked at the ground. "I talked to Dean Mack today." He paused and peeked up at her.

She scoffed. "Dean Mack isn't exactly the most reliable source of information." The scoundrel could lie to a priest while looking him in the eyes and putting his hand on the Bible. He had been one of her least favorite classmates.

"Granted. But he was a sergeant."

She gave an unladylike snort. "And he got demoted for lying on his conscription papers, if I remember right."

"Clara, would you listen to me?"

She forced herself to meet his gaze. "Fine. What did *Sergeant* Mack tell you?"

Edward swallowed. "Everyone who's coming home is home. Or accounted for, at least."

She bit her lip so hard she tasted blood.

"Clara," he said softly, taking a step closer. "Do you... do you ever wonder what comes next? I mean, when we're done waiting for James?"

"You mean after he's back?"

"I mean when... *if* he doesn't come back. What then?"

Clara's throat tightened, but before she could rebuke him for such thoughts, he took a step backward.

"It's not just me, Clara. Everyone is saying it."

"Everyone is saying what?" Clara put her hands on her hips, not nearly as cold as she had been a moment ago.

Edward ran his hands down his face. "This is coming out all wrong," he muttered. Then he took another big breath. "Look, you've been as faithful as an angel. But it's been a year and a half. Just... just say for a moment that he's not coming back. Just pretend. What then?"

Tears ran down her face.

"Because as much as we hate it," he said, his voice cracking, "you and I both know that's at least a possibility."

How she wanted to deny it. She needed to deny it. But even now, as she pressed her fist against her mouth and tried to force his words out of her head, a sob escaped her chest.

Edward put his hands on his head as he looked out at the alleyway behind her house. "And you and me, we go back a long way, too. We might not make a bad team." He looked back at her, his brown eyes warm and pleading. "We haven't these past few years."

"What are you saying?" she whispered.

He took her hands in his. They were surprisingly warm and very large. But their calluses were all wrong, and his fingers were too thick. Not like the lean, quick fingers she had come to know so well.

He spoke slowly. "I'm saying, I know I'm not James. I'll never be. No one can fill those shoes. But if you could like me even half as much as you loved him, I'd be a happy man."

This wasn't happening. It was all wrong. James was supposed to be here. Edward was supposed to be his faithful follower, and the three of them were supposed to be friends forever. They had been that way since they were small. But Edward without James?

Edward hurried on. "My father's going to give me the farm soon. He says I'm ready, and he can't keep it up anymore. I've already got a house, and you'd have everything you could ever need."

Clara turned away and breathed slowly as she tried to wrap her head around the idea. Edward was good enough to make any father-in-law proud. He was thoughtful and hard working. Whoever he married would be warm and comfortable as long as she lived.

But he wasn't James. His figure was too solid, and he didn't have any cleft in his jaw. He didn't spend his days dreaming of all the places the army could take him, and he definitely did not enjoy arguing just for the fun of it the way Clara liked.

"I wouldn't ask you to stop caring for him." Edward's voice broke through her thoughts. "I'll care for him until I die, and I'd never try to take from you what he gave, but…. Look, I'm not going to ask you to say yes tonight. In fact, I'm not even going to ask you to be my girl. But just think about it." His warm, hopeful eyes probed hers. "Promise?"

Could she do it? Could she love Edward? Could she ever admit that James might truly be gone? And if he was, like her mother suggested, would he have wanted her to stay alone and sad forever?

Unfortunately, she knew the answer all too well.

"Clara?" Edward whispered.

"Okay," she said in a weak whisper.

His face broke into a relieved grin, but she turned away. "I-I think I need to be alone."

"Oh. Of course."

The screen door opened, and a third set of footsteps joined them.

"But before you go, son…" came Drosselmeyer's voice. The warm coat was lifted from her shoulders, and the cold evening air assaulted her through the beautiful but thin dress. Her godfather handed him the coat, not bothering to hide the disdain in his voice. "You'll need this." A new coat that smelled of tobacco was draped over her shoulders in the place of Edward's, and she clutched it close as the door shut behind her.

"I never liked him." Her godfather leaned over the railing beside her and looked into the alley.

She gave him a skeptical look. "You've known him for less than an hour."

"Which is more than enough time to suss out his character." Drosselmeyer sniffed and tried to flick a piece of fuzz from his shirt.

She rested her head on his shoulder. "You miss James, too, don't you?"

"I do. He was a good boy, and he was always up to just enough mischief to be fun." Drosselmeyer fixed her with a studious gaze, "But I also miss the way you used to smile when he entered the room. You used to get so excited talking about all the things you were going to do together. California, if I remember right. The Grand Canyon." He looked at the ground. "You don't talk much about the future anymore."

She shrugged. "I figured getting through each day was enough of a battle."

"Fair enough. Of course...." He reached into his pocket and pulled out a cigar and studied it for a moment before scowling. "I'll say this about your boy as well. At least he knew how to cut a cigar properly. None of this little nub business." He shook his head and shoved the cigar back in his pocket. "I asked that Fredward, or whatever his name is, to trim my cigar, and he practically cut the thing in half."

"Do you think I ought to move on?" Clara wasn't usually keen on asking men questions regarding love or romance, but Drosselmeyer was different from most men. He was different from most people. And never once had he told her that she needed to hurry and grow up.

"Mourning is a complicated thing. No one can tell you exactly how to do it or when it should be done."

"Then you think he's gone, too." She hadn't known that her heart could fall any further down in her chest, but apparently, it could.

"I never said that. I was merely acknowledging that you shouldn't rush into that boy's proposal."

She stiffened. "Edward wasn't proposing."

"His proposal to propose. Whatever he was doing, it's not something you need to do to pacify your mother."

Clara gaped. "How did you know about the conversation with my mother?"

Drosselmeyer snorted. "Who do you think she comes and talks to when your father is gone and she's thought herself into a frenzy?"

"Oh." She leaned forward to glimpse the sky. "I wish it would snow."

"You hate the snow." Drosselmeyer folded his hands and leaned back to study her with his piercing gray eyes. "What do you really wish for, Clara?" When she didn't answer immediately, he gave her a gentle nudge. "Sometimes wishes change things, but not in the way you think." He leaned forward. "So what is it that you wish for?" he said again, more slowly this time. "The way you used to wish when you were a little girl."

"I wish...." She paused. Wishing that James could be there beside her was just another way to break her heart. She wanted so much to believe it could be true, but she had believed too much already. Every night, she'd gone to bed praying to wake up to news about the boy she loved. But tonight she just couldn't say. "I wish I knew the truth," she whispered slowly. "Then maybe I could move on like everyone wants me to."

"And if you decide you can't move on?"

She gave him a sad smile. "At least I'll know."

5

WISHES AND PRAYERS

As much as she wanted to stay outside, it was too cold. The rest of the evening was a blur. Some relatives, like her Uncle Jonathan and Cousin Rita, didn't know what to say when they encountered her in the hall. They either tried to make awkward small talk or dodged her as though there was an emergency in the next room. Others, such as her Uncle Thomas, Cousin Lucy, and Grandfather Theo, said too much, talking about the weather and her job, and the price of beans. Anything to avoid mentioning James. And then there was Edward. He vacillated between sending her nervous glances and joyous beams for the rest of the evening.

They all meant well, all except for maybe Marla, but all Clara wanted was the warmth of her own bed in the dark of night where she could lie in the moonlight and trace her little nutcracker's familiar features until she fell into a dreamless sleep.

After what felt like years of supper and exchanging gifts and far too much talk about politics, the guests began to leave. Each of them wished Clara and her family a Merry Christmas as they left, most avoiding Clara's direct gaze. Only her Aunt Pearl and Drosselmeyer met her eyes.

"Don't you listen to Marla." Aunt Pearl scowled in the direction of Aunt Marla's car. "That woman could out-sour a lemon."

Clara gave her aunt a grateful smile and a kiss as she said goodbye, then turned to Drosselmeyer. Her godfather reached down for one last hug and whispered in her ear. "If I ever had a daughter, I couldn't have wished for one better than you." He pulled back just enough to look deeply into her eyes.

She was a little surprised and saddened to see how ancient those eyes suddenly looked.

"I'm going to do my very best to get you that Christmas miracle."

She gave him a wry smile. "I don't think a wish like that is something you can wrap up in a box."

Drosselmeyer's eyes gleamed. "That's why it's called a miracle." And with that, he put on his hat and left.

"What do you think he meant by that?" her father said.

Clara shook her head. She was as mystified as anybody. But then, Drosselmeyer was a mysterious man, and that was one of the greatest reasons she loved him.

As soon as the house was clear, Clara's mother chased her out of the entryway and sent her up for a bath and bed. She would have argued, but the thought of cleaning dishes was a little more than she could handle, and as she trudged up the stairs, she realized she was as exhausted as her mother had said.

But when her head hit the pillow, she was unable to fall asleep. So she did what she did every night and pulled the small wooden picture frame from under her pillow. The photo belonged on her bedside table, but after her conversation with her mother, Clara had decided it was safest out of sight. Now, however, as the silence roared in her ears, in the weak light of a single candle, she traced the shape of his face.

She'd gone giddy the day James gave her the portrait. For though she'd known him nearly all her life, that picture changed him, at least in her mind, from a boy into a man. A sense of naughtiness caught her when she first gazed at the photo, for it was almost as if she, an engaged woman, was gazing at someone other than her fiancé.

James had always been cocky. He would try any trick, at least once or twice, and he played most sports. His blue eyes often twinkled over some harmless mischief he was planning. But where the boy had been cocky, the man in this picture was confident. She could see it in the sharp angles of his shoulders and the perfect posture of his neck. Clear, serious eyes stared back at her from behind the glass. His clean-shaven face was not unusual, but his short hair was nearly invisible under his hat. And though he had always kept a lean build, his arms had filled out some, as had his chest. Gold pins, two guns crossed at the center, held down his jacket lapels, and two more pins that said *U.S.* held down his jacket collar. The photo made her ache to hold him all the more.

As the clouds darkened the sky, and the photograph's details became difficult to see, her mind drifted back to the day he proposed.

The late spring day had been cold and blustery, her least favorite kind of day to be outside. The kind of day that made her nose run and her eyes water and ruined her hair until she washed it again. But after much coaxing, pleading, and threatening to tell her mother about one of their childhood pranks, James had finally convinced her to accompany him to the baseball field.

"Well," she called over the wind. "You got what you wanted. I'm here. Now, what's this all about?"

James surprised her by pulling a plate of cookies and a pitcher of lemonade from the basket he had brought with him.

He tilted his chin up and grinned as he set them on the lid of the picnic basket. "I made the cookies myself."

"Chocolate chip. You have my attention." She lifted a cookie with a flirtatious smile and bit down. She immediately, however, regretted her big bite, for, without a doubt, James had confused sugar with salt.

About the time Clara began to cough and sputter, so did James. They grabbed for the pitcher of lemonade at the same time and managed to tip it over and spill it on both of them.

Cold and sticky was not her idea of fun, but James looked so flummoxed that she couldn't help laughing. She laughed until she cried, and every time she looked at him, his scowl grew, and she started laughing all over again.

After five minutes of hysterical laughing on her part, and lots of grumbling and scowling on James's, she was finally able to close the picnic basket and put it on the ground. She leaned over and planted a kiss on his cheek.

"Now, what did you drag me out here and baptize me with lemonade for?" She expected some sort of saucy reply about winning a bet with his sister, or something to that effect, but instead, his smile disappeared. He stared at the ground and ran a hand through his thick, brown hair.

"You know all those plans we keep talking about? With kids, and a house and a dog, and all that?"

Her heart beat a little unevenly, but she managed to keep her face neutral. "I do."

"Well, I figured now that we're eighteen, it was time to get started on those dreams." He paused and glanced up at her, an unnamable emotion in his blue eyes. "So I enlisted this morning."

As he was speaking, she'd hopped off the fence and dug around in the basket in hopes he'd remembered to pack some blankets. But at the mention of his enlistment, she froze, hand still in the basket. She took a moment before she could bring herself to meet his eyes.

"Aw, come on now." He jumped off the fence and crouched down in front of her, his eyes pleading. "You knew I always wanted to join the military. And I figure this way, we can get married like we've been planning to. If we do it before I leave, you'll have all the money you need to get by while I'm gone. You can even help your parents out if they need anything. And as soon as I get back, we'll take a late honeymoon. We'll go wherever you want." He gently pulled her hands from the basket and held them.

His fingers were rough from his work on Edward's farm, where he worked every day after school, but his hands were warm. But not warm enough to thaw the fear encasing her heart.

She was no war expert, but she'd seen enough films at the theater and read enough newspapers to know what kind of danger American soldiers were facing. Sure, his dreams of being a soldier had been fun when they were children, back when he could run and pretend to fight the Central Powers with guns made of sticks and grenades made of rotten apples. But even as she'd held his hands in that moment, she tried to imagine one of those grenades headed for him.

She must have flinched because the next thing she felt were his fingers gently brushing her cheek.

The wind had died down enough she heard his whisper. "Hey, hey there. Who knows? I may get stuck behind some desk at Fort Bragg. Then you can come see me, and I'll get the best of both worlds."

"Or you could get sent across the ocean—"

"I'd rather enlist than get drafted."

His words were soft as he pulled her to her feet and into his chest. The cold air made the tears on her cheeks sting, and she buried her face in his shirt. "I want to feel like doing the right thing was my choice, rather than an obligation."

She knew him well enough not to argue. And deep down, she knew that if she'd been in his shoes, she would have wanted the same thing. But that didn't make what they were about to face any easier.

"Just think," he said, nuzzling her ear, "maybe we'll get lucky before I go, and when I come back and this war's all over, I'll have two beautiful people to come home to."

This only made her cry harder.

He held her tight and spoke into her hair. "Unfortunately, I'll be shipping out to training pretty soon. That probably means you won't be able to have that big fancy wedding you've been planning since you were five."

She shook her head fiercely. "It doesn't matter."

He paused and looked down at her. "It doesn't?"

"No." She glared at him as she wiped her face on her arm. "Because we can't get married."

For the first time, fear flickered in his eyes. "What do you mean?"

She stepped back and folded her arms across her chest. "You haven't asked me to marry you."

He stared at her for a long moment before pinching the bridge of his nose and muttering something about being a fathead. Then he knelt and reached into the basket once more. He stayed on his knee and opened his hand to reveal a little golden band with a square blue diamond in the center and little white diamonds surrounding it.

"Clara Marie Frost," he said, taking her hand once more, "will you marry me?"

And in that moment, as she said yes and threw her arms around his neck, despite all she knew they were about to face, she had been happy. Truly and utterly happy. She was going to marry her childhood sweetheart, and as much as it pained her, he could do what was right and fight for those who couldn't fight for themselves.

But as sweet as his plans had sounded that day on the baseball field, they began to disintegrate almost as soon as she'd said yes. To begin with, Clara's mother had refused to attend a courthouse wedding.

"At least wait a week so we can have something in the church!" her mother had pleaded tearfully when she heard of their plans.

And though waiting made James nervous, Clara was glad they'd waited when she saw all the ribbons and flowers her mother and aunts used to decorate the church. It would be a small ceremony. But it would be hers.

That was, until the pastor fell sick on the morning of the ceremony, and James was called away to training the next day. A slot had opened up, the recruiter said, and James was next in line. And so with a quick kiss and a mournful look at her single-banded ring, James left in the dark of early morning the day they should have been married.

In a way, she'd been living in that day ever since.

Clara closed her eyes in an attempt to shut out the thoughts of what should have been. She didn't mean to fall asleep, so the boom of the grandfather clock in the hall jerked her awaken from her half-slumber. But just as she was about to go back to sleep, she remembered her nutcracker downstairs.

After throwing on a robe, she stumbled down the dark hall. What would have happened, she wondered for the millionth time as she padded down the hardwood floor. What if they'd been married as planned, and she hadn't let her mother talk them out of a courthouse wedding? Would she have gotten pregnant right away? Raising a child without a father would be terrible enough during those early years, let alone for his or her entire life. But at least she would've had some part of him to keep with her forever, something more than a photograph and a ring.

The grandfather clock boomed again so loudly she nearly tripped down the stairs. Her ears were still ringing by the time she reached the main floor, but she ignored them and set to looking for her nutcracker.

It had to be downstairs. The last time she remembered seeing it was when her godfather had wrapped his handkerchief around its jaw. He wouldn't have taken her gift without telling her. But no matter how much she tried reasoning, her fragile sense of calm began to unravel into panic as she searched. But just before she began to despair that one of her younger cousins must have taken it, a strange sound came from what sounded like the back door.

Tiptoeing through the kitchen, she peered out the back window. Snow was falling and quickly blanketing the ground, but that wasn't what made her gasp.

Drosselmeyer was on his back porch, which was not unusual. He often liked to have a smoke outside on cool evenings. But he was hunched over the railing, his face contorted in what looked like pain. From the way he was leaning against the railing, she was sure his toppling over it was not a matter of if, but when. She sprinted to the front of the house, grabbed her shoes, and dashed out the back door.

"Godfather!" she called, wincing as cold air hit her face. "Are you hurt?" She darted up his back porch and threw an arm around his back. "And what are you doing out here in the middle of the night?"

Drosselmeyer grimaced but refused to lean into her. He groaned and shoved her hands away. "You don't have much time!"

She ignored his efforts and pulled him into a chair.

"Leave me be!" He coughed, falling back into the cushions. "Go to him!"

"Who?" Clara stared at him. Should she wake her parents?

Drosselmeyer pointed down the alley. "Him!"

She looked to where he was pointing, down the alley on the other side of her.

In the newly fallen snow were four figures. One was on the ground, and the other three standing over him were not attempting to help. She ran to the edge of the porch to get a better look. Should she scream for her father or call the police?

Then the man on the ground rolled over. And when she caught a glimpse of his face, her heart stopped beating.

She bolted down the porch steps and went flying across the snow-dusted backyard. Sense caught up with her heart, however, and she stopped short of the men.

The three men were hunched over and all dressed in black. One stepped into the light of the moon, just enough for Clara to make out shiny black boots.

She was strong compared to most women, but she would be no match for them, no matter how hard she hit. Fighting the men, whoever they were, was not an option. But if she could use the element of surprise, just maybe….

She looked around to find something to use to scare them off. The first thing she noticed was that her neighbors had stacked a large pile of tin cans in the alley to donate to the war effort before it ended. Then she spotted Fritz's baseball bat leaned against the edge of her porch. If she could throw the bat at the cans, it would create a ruckus. But when she stepped into a small snowdrift, some spilled into her shoe.

Shoes would fly better than bats.

Leaning against the porch, she removed her shoe and said a prayer as she took aim. Then she threw the shoe.

The shoe hit the pile of cans with a tremendous crash. The

three men in black jumped and looked around wildly. Two of them darted into the night before the cans even finished scattering, but the third stood his ground. For one petrifying moment, he looked directly into her eyes. Then he gave her the slightest grin before following his friends.

She stood frozen in place as she watched them go, and she might have remained that way if not for the unmistakably familiar groan coming from the man on the ground.

She stumbled toward him in the snow, pausing only to grab her shoe and slip it back on as she fell at his side. She trembled as she gently took his face in her hands.

"James," Clara whispered.

She was dreaming. She had to be. How else did she explain her fiancé being attacked by three ruffians in the alley behind her house? The fiancé who had disappeared in Europe, no less. And yet, here she was, touching his face, tracing the same lines and angles she'd known all her life. He still wore his olive-drab uniform and heavy brown boots, and his hair was cut close to his scalp. Oddly, his usually clean-cut face was covered in shadowy stubble. A few unfamiliar scars crossed his cheeks, neck, and forehead, and new lines crinkled the corners of his eyes and mouth. But without a doubt, it was him. Something akin to common sense said she should help him back onto the porch, for she was mildly aware of the wet snow seeping through her nightgown, but all she could do was stare at him, frozen in place and time.

"James?" Her voice rose with fear as he stayed still in her arms, his eyes shut. "James?"

Just as she was about to start screaming for someone to help them, his chest rose and his blue eyes fluttered open and settled on her. He smiled at her, looking sweet and tired, but as the sleep cleared from his eyes, his lips parted, and his eyes widened. He sat straight up. Then, as he scrambled to his feet, pulling her with him, he grabbed her shoulders and his eyes frantically searched hers. With one hand, he traced the shape of her face while he buried the other in her hair.

"Clara!" His words sounded strangled and uneven. "Are you—how?"

She was breathing so hard she could barely laugh for joy. But it didn't matter. Because James was here. He was here and breathing and holding her tightly as though she might run away from him. As if she could ever walk, let alone run from him.

His thumb came dangerously close to her lips, and she leaned in closer. His jacket smelled of... well, she couldn't tell what it smelled like. There were too many scents to name one. She didn't have time to examine him any further, though, because he closed the remaining distance between them and before she could react, he was pressing his lips against hers.

His kiss sent a wave of heat from her lips to her chest, and she clung to him as he pressed his hand against the small of her back. He was taller than she remembered, and his chest and arms had filled out in ways that sent shivers across her shoulders.

As he kissed her, she tried to remember all the sentimental things she had planned to tell him. Not a night had gone by when she didn't imagine their reuniting. And in those fantasies, she thought up a hundred clever, romantic things to say. Now, though, as he crushed her against his chest, she couldn't think of a single one. Her mind was spinning like a broken record.

He's home.

He's alive.

He's home.

His other hand moved from her face to her shoulders, to her neck and back up to her face, as though she might disappear at any moment, and he kept whispering the beginnings of sentimental thoughts, but he never got more than a few words out before beginning again. She did, however, make out the gentle way he uttered her name over and over again between the fragments.

"Clara. Clara. Clara." Each word was a caress, blending in her mind with the way he was holding her gently, yet fervently. And each word made her squeeze tighter as she wrapped her arms around him and pressed against his chest.

Much too soon, though, he pulled back, his brows drawn quizzically. "But how did you get here?"

"What do you mean?" In her elation, she could hardly find words to speak, despite the wet snow seeping into her shoes. "We're here. At my house."

He looked around as though just noticing his surroundings. Then he turned his gaze back to her, his expression softening into a gentle smile. "You are so beautiful," he breathed, tucking a lock of hair behind her ear.

She leaned closer again in anticipation, but before their lips met, his eyes flicked over her shoulder, and he froze. He grabbed her hand and pulled her against the wall into the deepest part of the shadow, out of the moonlight that was now bright and free of clouds. "They brought you here, too?" The deep timbre of his voice was intoxicating.

She laughed nervously. "No one brought me here. I told you, we're at my house." She leaned in. "The question is how did *you* get here?" She peered down the street, trying to catch a glimpse of whoever might have dropped him off. "And why didn't the army tell us you were—"

"Stop."

"What?"

"Stop talking," he hissed. His grip on her arm tightened, and he kept her pressed against the wall. "They're here."

Clara stared at him. "Who?"

He swallowed and continued to scan their surroundings. "Did you see the rats?"

"The rats?"

He nodded, his jaw tight. "The Nazis that were following me?"

She shuddered again, this time, from the memory of the man in the shiny black books. And from the look in James's sharp eyes, he noticed. "The muggers?" She tried to make her voice light. "James, you're in Eagle Head, North Carolina. How on earth would Nazis have followed you all the way over here?" She paused. "And why are you calling them rats?"

He let out a gusty breath and buried his face in his hand. "Great."

She moved away from the wall to stand directly in front of him. "Come inside. We'll wake my parents and tell them about the muggers. Father will know what to do." She took his hand and squeezed it. "You're home," she said in a softer voice, drinking in every bit of him as he stood in front of her. But to her surprise, instead of smiling back or looking relieved, he shook his head.

"I've been fighting this war for too long." His grip tightened, and he took a step closer. "I'm not going to let them drag you into this, too!"

Clara blinked. "I don't know who those men were, but the war ended three months ago." How did he not know this? Especially if he was home. The voyage across the Atlantic wasn't a short trip one might nap through by accident.

As she watched him study the alley behind them, something akin to fear niggled at her mind, the feeling that something wasn't right as he glowered into the darkness. She tugged him toward the door. "It's Christmas Eve," she said. "Let's go inside. We'll call the police, and we'll work this all out."

A look of longing touched his face as he glanced down and

seemed to take in her nightgown for the first time. Then he frowned.

She looked down, too, but instead of her snowy side yard, she stood on a street. Her shoes had dried, and she gasped as her nightgown changed into Aunt Pearl's blue dress right before her eyes. "What in the world…." When she looked up to see why he hadn't answered her, she found him again scanning their surroundings. And just as her nightgown had turned into something new, so had her neighborhood. Gone was her brick house with its blue trimming and the houses of her neighbors as well.

Instead, where the familiar snow-dusted gingerbread-like houses had stood in neat, clean lines, she and James were standing on a wide stone street across from a large building with red window frames beneath a slanted roof. Dirty snow was piled up against the building and at the edges of the street. Raucous laughter floated from the open door as several American soldiers stumbled out, girls on their arms. Though the street was dark, for the moon had disappeared along with her house, the lights inside were bright. The chaotic sounds of off-key Christmas carols drifted out the front door.

Clara's knees buckled and she would have fallen if James hadn't caught her. Her head swam as she clutched his sleeve and tried to stand again. What was wrong with her? She had never lost her mind, at least that she was aware of, but what if the anxiety of the evening had pushed her over the edge of sanity?

"What just happened?" she whispered.

Instead of answering, he took her hand and pulled her toward the building with the red window frames, throwing one more wary glance behind them. "Come on. We need to get you inside."

6

TRUST ME

"**W**hy?" Clara panted as he hurried her across the street.

"They don't come out in public. They'll watch, but they never attack in places with more than two or three witnesses."

"Who?" She tried to make sense of what he was saying, but the fact that they had just traveled between worlds and the familiar sensation of his hand in hers was more than a little distracting.

And yet, as her sense of equilibrium returned, her heart broke. It had all seemed so real at first. He was there with her, just the way she had prayed for years. And he seemed so real. The way he smelled, the feel of his fingers intertwined with hers. But now....

This was a dream. It had to be. She was with James. In the middle of the night. Without a clue as to where she was. And if she looked closely enough over her shoulder, she was able to make out the silhouettes of men scurrying after them, darting from shadow to shadow.

"James?" Dream or not, she leaned in closer and shivered, but not from the cold. "Behind us—"

"Keep moving," he said tersely. "They won't follow us inside."

He put his hand on her back, and she relaxed a little. The gesture was so reassuring, so familiar, it made her want to cry and laugh at the same time. This was a cruel dream, teasing her with her greatest desires, and she was playing right into its clutches. She was letting him touch her, following his directions, hanging on his every glance and every word. And what would she have to show for it in the morning but a splotchy face and a Christmas full of longing for what she could never have?

She should wake up. She should put this foolishness away before it broke her heart. Especially since it was more real than any dream she'd ever experienced before. But could she wake up now? Wasn't the surefire heartbreak worth another hour in his presence?

She had suffered through countless dreams that seemed as real as day, dreams when he came home, and they lived their happily ever after. Every one of those dreams had resulted in a day of hiding the stinging in her eyes and the feeling of death in her heart. Because every time she woke up, she lost him all over again. And this, by far, was the most tangible dream she'd ever had.

"Almost there." James's voice jarred her from her inner turmoil.

They were close enough to make out the sign, which said, The Red Lion. Light from the inside spilled through the red door. The thick beams inside were painted black against the whitewashed walls.

"Where are we?" She had to shout over the noise as they walked through the door.

"I can't hear you!" He pointed at the piano in the corner, on which three or four people were banging at the same time, hollering Christmas carols at the top of their lungs. He pulled her away from the entrance, and shoved his way through groups of giggling women and shouting, laughing men to the bar in the back of the room. When they reached the bar, Clara was thankful to find that it was quiet enough she could hear herself think.

The barkeep stood behind the bar, a middle-aged man with gray hair and an unenthusiastic expression. His apron was dirty, and he was wiping down the far end of the counter.

"I said, where are we?" If she was going to be stubborn and refuse to wake up, she might as well make the best of it by soaking up as much of his voice as she could. Because tomorrow she would pay.

"England," he said. "After we finished up in Sicily, we came back to England to prepare for Normandy."

She stopped. "Wasn't Normandy when—"

"Sit here." He gestured to a stool and took the seat beside her. "We don't know how long they'll let us stay. Might as well get something to eat and drink while we're here."

She hopped up on the barstool. "Wait, what do you mean let us stay? And who are those men following us?" She shuddered again.

James scanned the crowd once more, but she noticed his eyes continually going back to the windows. "Nazis. But not the usual kind." He straightened his shoulders and sat taller. "There's been talk of Hitler's... obsession." He finally looked at her directly, and the weight of his clear blue eyes threatened to undo her nerves, which were precariously balanced between elation and terror. "Have they reported on it at home yet?"

"Hitler?" she echoed.

James nodded before returning to his surveillance. "Word has it that Hitler's been getting into all sorts of dark stuff."

She snorted. "Like trying to exterminate entire races isn't dark."

"I mean it. Things like witchcraft, and all other sorts of unholy things."

Clara tried to laugh off the absurdity of his claim, but her giggle came out more strangled than convincing. "James, there's no such thing as witchcraft."

James leaned down and pointed to the window closest to them. "Then explain that."

Clara was about to scold him for believing in such silliness when her gaze came to rest on a pair of glowing yellow eyes staring through the glass. They were trained on her.

She shrieked and threw herself at James, toppling off her barstool in the process. He caught her, despite the awkwardness of her leap, and once she was back on her barstool, he stood and wrapped his arms around her, pressing her into his chest. She leaned into him, trembling as he rubbed her back in fast, firm circles. His uniform was thick, but even through it, he was warm, and she snuggled even closer. When she was brave enough to peek at the window again, against her better judgment, the eyes were gone.

"What was that?" she whimpered, clinging to his shirt.

"Those are the Nazis I was talking about," James said, still rubbing her back and as he held her against him. "No one else can see them but me." His rubbing briefly slowed, then sped even faster. "And, apparently, now you."

"But what are they?"

He shrugged without letting go of her. "Hitler's creations is all I can guess. I can't come up with any other explanation."

"But the war...." Her voice faltered when she had the courage to lean back and look at him. "It's over. Hitler's dead." Her statement came out like more of a question than a fact.

James let out a harsh laugh. "Is that what the news told you over there?" He motioned to the room full of American GIs surrounding them. "Does this look like the war is over?

Because if it is, someone needs to tell all these boys they can go home."

Clara looked around. He was right. Why were so many uniformed Americans in a British pub?

"I don't know how," James said as he sat down, still gripping her hand, "but they've managed to sneak into Britain, and no one, not the Brits or the Americans, knows about it but me."

Clara drummed on the counter with her fingers as she looked around again. "What do you mean?" The soldiers around them were Americans, to be sure, but none of them seemed to sense the threat James did. Then it occurred to her. "Wait, how many times have you been here?"

He was eyeing the bartender. "Don't know."

"You don't know?"

He shook his head.

She sat back and studied him. "Then, how long have you been seeing these Nazis?" What had he called them earlier? Rats?

"It's hard to tell." He frowned as though he hadn't considered it before. "They don't stay still very long. We move a lot."

Clara stared at him, unable to make any sense of it. How could he not know how long he'd been running? Or how many times he'd been to England? Or even that the war was over? But then, maybe it wasn't supposed to make sense. After all, they'd just been transported across the Atlantic to a pub in England. This was all only a dream.

Her heart clenched up in her chest so hard it was painful.

"But..." She shook her head. "I thought you were supposed to be jumping out of airplanes wherever the army sent you. Why are you following Nazis around? Or are they following you?" If this was a dream, she was ridiculously tired. Had she slept at all?

He gave her that funny look again. "Now that you ask, I'm

not sure." His eyes darkened, and he straightened his shoulders. "I don't know, but I do know that this fight is between me and them. I came here to fight, and for them to drag me around the world is one thing. But to get you involved…." His jaw twitched. "They've gone too far this time." He began to stand, and a silent alarm went off in Clara's head. He had that same look in his eyes as the day he'd decked Arthur Smith in fifth grade when Arthur tripped Clara and made her cry.

"Wait." She put her hand on his chest. "Where are you going?"

"I'm going to take care of this." His eyes were already on the door, and Clara panicked. Dream or not, she wasn't ready to watch him get killed. She racked her brains for a way to keep him inside, and almost immediately came up with a solution. It was cowardly, of that she was aware. But it was something he wouldn't be able to resist.

She grabbed his wrist as he began to go. "Please, don't leave me!" When he turned back to her, she tried to shrink as small as she could. "I don't know anyone here, I don't know how to get home." The tears she'd considered faking, however, suddenly felt quite real. "If something happens to you, what am I going to do?" When he still didn't move, she whimpered. "At least finish telling me what you started." Being alone, she could handle. Watching him die was another matter entirely.

His expression became pained and his jaw worked a mile a minute, the way it always did when he wasn't sure about something. But finally, to her great relief, he nodded.

"Give me a minute to do something first."

He went to the windows and began to pull their shades down. He'd finished half the pub before she realized what he was doing.

She glanced around. Would anyone be annoyed? But everyone else seemed too drunk or distracted to pay him or the covered windows any attention. When they were all closed, he came back and motioned to the bartender. "The usual for me. And a plate of whatever's on the stove." He looked at her. "What would you like, Clara?"

He had a usual? Once again her suspicions were aroused, but she did her best to smile at the bartender. "Just a rootbeer, please." Then she looked back at James. "So at least tell me the last time you remember being with your division."

James took her hand and played absently with the ring on her finger. "The last thing I remember... before all this at least," he waved at the surrounding scene, "was when we were going to make a jump in France. The jump was a success. The battle started hard, but...." He shook his head. "After that, I woke up and found myself here in England. Along with the rats."

Clara couldn't have moved if she'd wanted to. "What did they want?"

He looked up at the old wooden beams stretching over their heads, and his voice dropped to a whisper. "I could see the red on their uniforms even in the dark. That's when I realized I didn't have my gun, just my knife." He lifted a pant leg just enough to show her the knife hidden beneath.

She shivered again.

"I fought for my life that night. There were three, maybe four of them. They nearly killed me, but thanks to all the crap the army put me through, I was able to fend them off."

She gripped the edge of her chair so hard her knuckles turned white, but she didn't care. "What happened then?"

James bit his lip, and for a moment, she was reminded of the little boy she'd loved since first grade. So much about him had changed. The way he carried himself. The way his eyes shone a little too brightly when he talked about the Nazis. The lines on his face that made him look ten years older instead of just three. But that expression reminded her that beneath the hardened soldier, the little boy still lived underneath. "They ran. I ran. We've been chasing each other ever since."

Clara frowned. "Where?"

"Everywhere. Italy. Fort Bragg. Then England again." He shrugged. "Always somewhere I'm familiar with at least. Going someplace I don't know the layout of…." He shook his head. "That would be bad."

"But if you're going back and forth between continents, then how are you getting there?" She looked down at her shoes, remembering her own trip here. But this was just a dream. And yet, she wanted to know. She wanted to push him into thinking clearly like the James she knew. As if that might make him come back in real life.

Stupid girl.

This was the most specific dream she had ever experienced. It was also the cruelest situation her rebellious mind could have conjured up in her sleep.

James was quiet for a minute while he stroked her fingers. Dark stubble covered his angular jaw, but his lips looked warmer and more inviting than ever before, and as she watched them, Clara realized their first kiss hadn't been nearly long enough. He'd been so busy dragging her away from the rats that there'd been no time for more. But the rats couldn't get them, and with the windows covered, she no longer needed to worry about beady, yellow eyes watching them from afar. And she wanted more.

He must have been thinking the same thing, because the moment she moved closer, he was there, too.

"I've missed you, Clara Frost," he whispered, brushing his mouth against hers. "I would have given up long ago if I didn't have you to get home to."

A thrill rippled through her stomach, and she closed her eyes in anticipation. But as soon as his hand had reached up to cup her jaw, someone cleared his their throat.

"If you're going to be that familiar, you might as well go out there with all of them," the barkeep grumbled. He nodded at the loud patrons gathered around the piano. "Where I don't have to watch you."

Clara blushed profusely and muttered an apology, but only when they were properly back on their own stools did the barkeep walk away.

A wry smile on his face, James leaned back, but his eyes were hungry as he continued to hold her gaze, the intensity of his eyes drawing her like a moth to blue flames.

"Where is this again?" Clara asked, her face still hot from both the reproach in the older man's face and the desire written clearly on James's.

"This was one of my favorite places whenever we got time away from the base." James signaled the barkeep. "I thought we ordered some drinks."

The barkeep rolled his eyes, but he pulled a glass bottle from the shelf behind him and poured them each a drink in a tall glass.

Clara took hers and studied it. The liquid was brown, and the top was frothy. She sniffed it and grimaced. It smelled like burnt rubber. "I don't think this is root beer."

James gave her a wicked grin. "Just taste it."

"This isn't like when you tricked me into drinking a cup full of vanilla, is it?"

"You remember that?" He beamed.

She stuck her tongue out at him. "Of course I do. It was awful!"

"Yeah, my mom was pretty peeved at me, too." He took a long swig of the stuff in the glass. "I had to paint the entire fence to pay for all that vanilla." He took another drink and grinned. "But it was worth it."

Clara had a smart retort on her tongue when a group of pretty blonde girls caught her eye.

"What is it?" He followed her gaze to the girls, who were staring, unabashed.

"They're rather brave." She glared back at them. "They haven't stopped looking at you since they walked in."

"Well, over here, American GIs have somewhat of a reputation." He looked at her glass. "You're not going to drink that, are you?"

She shoved it over to him.

He took a swig and wiped his mouth. "You see, us American guys get paid over five times what these poor British boys do. And when you're young and you've got no family to send money home to or responsibilities to pay for, it's easy to be generous." He shrugged and finished his second glass. "And the girls like that."

Clara was sure she didn't.

"Wait." He put his drink down and studied her. Then a delighted grin lit his face. "Are you jealous?"

She huffed. "Why should I be jealous? We only went steady all through school, and you put a ring on my finger as soon as you could afford one." She swished her hair at the posse of girls and turned back toward him, making sure her glare was deadly. "Why on earth would I be jealous?"

He laughed and took her cheeks in his hands, pulling her forward to place a kiss on her forehead. All of her irritation evaporated at the gesture, her heart lurching in her chest as she was reminded of just how good it felt. At the same time, the frightened little girl that lived deep inside her heart wondered how in the dickens she was going to wake up and continue living on as if this night had never happened.

He gestured at the four or five couples in the middle of the floor. Someone had cleared away several of the tables and created a space large enough for dancing.

"You wanna dance?"

"You don't dance."

"I do now." He stood and straightened his green jacket with dramatic flair.

She twisted her mouth and quirked an eyebrow. "Since when? You wouldn't even dance with me at prom."

"Ah, but I had a good teacher."

"I tried to teach you— "

"Clara Frost, I love you, but you couldn't lead anyone out of a box."

Clara opened her mouth to argue, but he was right. She was a terrible teacher. She folded her arms instead. "Alright then, who was this wonderful teacher?" She jerked her chin at the posse of blondes. "Was it one of those lovely ladies?"

When James left for the war, Clara made a deal with herself. She would never ask him about other women while he was gone, and she would never entertain the idea of him finding another. Because if she really sat down and thought about all the beautiful English and French girls he might encounter, or the very available nurses or USO performers he was likely to meet while he was gone, she would most surely lose her mind. As she watched the other girls now, though, she couldn't help but wonder if such a decision had been naïve.

But James just laughed, that deep belly laugh she remembered so well. It was good to see him really smiling, even if he was aggravating her on purpose.

"I don't think I'm going to tell you." He gave her another wicked grin. "You're cute when you're jealous."

"James!"

"Look! It's happening now! Your nose turns all red, and—"

But before he finished, the smile melted from his face and he stared at something behind her.

Clara turned and followed his gaze to the door, and her heart faltered.

A shadow with yellow eyes was watching from outside the open door as a group of drunk soldiers stumbled out of the bar, laughing loudly as they went.

"Alright, that's it." James growled deep in his throat as he glowered at the Nazi. "This ends now."

"But you said—"

But James was already shaking his head, that look of immovable determination in his eyes. "I want you to wait here for me. If you need anything, ask the barkeep. He's gruff, but a good man. And his wife is kind, too."

"But this still doesn't make any sense!" Clara reached for his jacket, barely managing to grab hold of his pocket. "Let's just slow down and... and form a plan!"

The look he gave her wasn't happy, but she took advantage of his pause.

"Look, something about this isn't right—"

"Obviously."

"Which," she said, "means there has to be a way out. A... a loophole or an escape or something. Maybe that's why I'm here! To change things!" She was grasping at straws, and she knew it. And from the look on his face, so did he. "Just don't make me lose you. Not again." Waking up would be hard enough. To wake up after watching him die, even in a dream, might be more than she could stand. Especially in a dream as real as this one.

She should really just wake herself up now. And yet... she couldn't do that. Not yet.

His eyes softened, and he took her hands in his. "And you won't have to. I'm done with this madness." His blue eyes blazed. "I'm going to deal with them. Then we're going home.

And I'm never leaving your side again." He kissed her forehead, and Clara wondered if it was possible to die of heartache.

"I promise," he whispered into her hair, pulling her against him once more. Then he leaned back and took her face in his hands. "Don't you trust me?"

"It's not you I don't trust," Clara whimpered. "It's them."

He gave her that ornery, crooked grin she loved so much, the one with the single dimple on the left side of his face. "I can do this. I'm going to do this. And we're going to have that fairy tale ending you always dreamed of."

When she hesitated, he sighed and pulled a piece of paper from his pocket. Unfolding it, he handed it to her. Through the fog in her eyes, Clara recognized her own writing. It was one of her letters.

"You said you thought I could do anything," he said quietly. "Did you believe that? Or were you just making it up?"

"What's going to be different this time," she said, "than all the times you've fought them before?"

His eyes tightened. "They involved you. This time, I want blood."

A half-sob nearly choked her, but she handed back the paper and nodded. She couldn't raise her voice above a whisper. "Then you'd better make it fast."

"Thank you. Now stay here."

She gave him a withering look, but he just returned it.

"Do you have hand-to-hand combat training?"

She had no answer for that, so she crossed her arms and wrinkled her nose to keep the tears at bay. He kissed her on the cheek once more before squaring his shoulders and stalking toward the door.

Clara had half a mind to follow him, but she remembered her father's warning from the time they'd found a mad dog in their backyard when she was small.

I know you want to help. But you're not big enough for this. If the dog came after you, I might get hurt trying to keep you safe.

James was right. She wasn't trained in hand-to-hand combat. She only surprised the Nazis with her shoe. She wouldn't have the first idea of what to do in a fight.

But as the minutes wore on, Clara became more and more uneasy. James was a good fighter. What he lacked in weight he made up for in agility and speed. And with the new muscles he had now, thanks to the army, he should be even better. But what was taking so long?

He should have been done by now. Fights were fast. She'd seen enough in the schoolyard when the boys got too big for their britches and challenged one another. Their brawls lasted a couple minutes at most. Unless…. Her stomach nearly heaved up the remnants of her supper.

Unless they were toying with him.

Unable to keep still any longer, Clara slid off her stool and wove her way through the other pub patrons to the nearest window.

When she peeked out into the dark street, there was just enough moonlight to see the fight. James was indeed doing well. Two of the four Nazis were on the ground, and James was circling with the third. But as he fell into a crouch, one of the Nazis on the ground swept his legs out from under him. Clara let out a little cry as he hit the ground hard.

7

FRIENDLY FIRE

*W*ithout a second thought, she tore through the crowd, shoving people out of her way as she ran to the door. Several cried out in protest, but she didn't pause until she was outside and had melted into the shadows. She had to take the Nazis by surprise as she had before. Unfortunately, she didn't have any more of an advantage this time than she had the first time. Maybe even less so. They knew she was here now.

By the time she got outside, two of the Nazis had fled. She crept closer, keeping her back to the pub's wall, and had nearly reached them when the Nazi still standing moved over to where James lay on the ground.

She screamed as he pulled a knife from his boot and held it above James.

At the sound of her shriek, the Nazi looked up, his yellow eyes meeting hers for half a second before something dark and fast slammed it to the ground.

Another form appeared at James's side and bashed the Nazi on the ground with the butt of his gun before grabbing James by the arms and pulling him over to Clara.

"You got him, Jones?" one of the dark forms said.

"Yeah," replied the other, "but I don't think he'll need my help for very long."

Clara couldn't see his face, but she heard a smile in his words. Still, she ignored him as she took in the blood trailing from James's nose and one of his ears.

"James?" She shook him. "James!"

"I've got a bloody nose. I'm not deaf." He scrunched up his eyes and coughed.

Clara was torn between smacking him and giving him the biggest kiss of his life as he sat up on his elbows and looked around. Then his eyes widened. "Jones! Kelly! What are you two fat-heads doing here?"

Only then did it dawn on Clara that someone besides them had also seen the Nazis. And whoever these two strangers were, they had come to help. As Clara tried to better study their helpers, she also realized that their little group was no longer on a dark British street. It was still night, but the moon was nearly as bright as day. And instead of standing behind the pub, they were in the middle of a field, surrounded by countless airplanes with dull green metal sides, rounded wingtips, and propellers wider as she was tall.

The one called Jones, a sturdy blond fellow with a scar across his jaw, bent down and helped James to his feet.

Thank goodness he could stand.

"Just had to ruin the evening, didn't you?" The other guy, Kelly, punched James in the shoulder and grinned. He had an even slighter build than James and a head of flaming red hair. He crossed his arms and shook his head, but the grin stayed.

James wiped the blood on his face with his sleeve and pulled Clara to his side with his other arm. "Clara, this is Robert Jones and Duff Kelly."

She smiled shyly and waved.

"This is the girl you've been telling us about?" Jones

scratched his head. "That picture you have doesn't do her justice."

"That picture is about to fall apart." James made a face.

Kelly elbowed him. "No wonder you challenged us all to a duel. I would, too, if my fiancé looked like that."

She raised her eyebrows. "Challenged everyone to a what?"

James turned red, which only made his friends roar with laughter.

"Your fiancé here," Jones clapped James on the shoulder, his brown eyes dancing, "had a little too much to drink one night. Pulled out your picture and showed it to everyone. When some bat crazy corporal said you weren't as pretty as his girl, he…." But he couldn't finish the story, he was laughing so hard.

Kelly picked up for him, a wicked grin on his face. "He picked up a butter knife from his dinner plate and challenged anyone to a duel who dared question your ultimate beauty."

By this time, Jones was laughing so hard he was crying.

"Oh, James." Clara rubbed her eyes, not sure if she should feel honored or give him a good scolding for drinking too much.

"I didn't actually do anything," James grumbled at the ground, shoving his hands in his pockets as they doubled over with laughter.

Jones snorted. "Yeah, because the colonel heard the whole thing and put you on spud duty in the kitchen for a week!"

"What else has he been up to while I've been gone?" Clara asked, fixing James with a look. This seemed a strange place to be standing around and teasing James, but she was nearly giddy with relief that the Nazis hadn't killed him in his fool-hearted attempt to defend her. Still, something was nagging at her, but she couldn't quite figure out what.

"Aw, you can't be mad at this guy," Kelly said when he was finally able to speak again. "He talked about you until everyone in the division was sick of hearing it. He went on and on about how pretty you were, and how you could outsmart any one of us."

Jones pulled a tube of M&Ms out of his pocket and popped a handful in his mouth. "Pretty soon we decided you sounded too good to be true, so we figured he'd just made you up."

"Well now you can all shut your pie holes," James said, putting an arm around Clara's shoulders, his grin smug. "Your proof is standing right in front of you." His grin widened. "In fact, Jones, I think you owe me a dollar." He held out his hand. "Pay up."

She smiled as the men squabbled over the bet they'd apparently made over her existence. Her chest felt warm as she realized that his affection for her had never waned after all. Not that she thought it had. And yet, there were nights when she'd wondered if the draw she held at home would be just as strong when they were apart.

Still, as the men shared insults, she couldn't suppress the feeling that something was off. It shouldn't be. After all, she was in a dream where her fiancé was whisked around the world by some unseen force where he faced his enemies over and over again. Anything could happen. Still, this moment seemed too perfect. This dream was the most lifelike she'd ever experienced. Could it get more real without blurring the lines between fantasy and reality? She glanced up at James's face. He was listening intently to whatever his friends were saying now, not a sign of doubt in his eyes.

But when Clara turned to hear what Kelly was saying, she realized that Jones was staring at her. And it wasn't the friendly gaze of a curious friend. His eyes were cold and unblinking. Then for a split second, so fast she wondered if she'd seen it at all, his brown eyes flashed yellow.

She shuddered and shrank into James's arms. Blinking

rapidly, it was a moment before she dared to look again. But when she did, nothing was amiss. Jones was listening to Kelly's story and laughing right along with James. Had she imagined it? Clara squeezed her eyes shut and rubbed them. She wouldn't be surprised. The sleep she was supposed to be getting didn't seem any closer than it had that afternoon at the grocer's.

"It sure left a hole when you disappeared," Kelly said to James, his smile fading. "The silence was pretty loud when no one was there to tell us about your girl."

Jones crossed his arms and stood taller. "What were you thinking tonight, taking those Jerries on by yourself?"

"What did you expect me to do?" James elbowed him. "I haven't had you jerks around for a long time."

"But you had your girl all to yourself in a cozy little pub." Kelly shook his head. "She even gave you all her beer, and you still had to take them head-on."

The smile in James's eyes died, and his arm tightened around her shoulder. "What did you say?"

Jones stopped laughing. "What's wrong, man?" He thumped him on the opposite shoulder. "We're just pulling your leg a bit. After—"

"No." James pushed Clara behind him.

Her skin prickled as she glanced at Kelly. He wasn't laughing either. But instead of looking intense like James or Jones, his mouth was twisted into a sneer, and his shoulders had begun to hunch.

"How did you know she gave me her beer?" James's voice grew hard. "Because the only way you would have seen that...." For one long second, they were all silent. Then James's eyes widened. He hauled back and slugged them both. They went down as he shoved Clara away. "Run, Clara! Run!"

As Clara turned to do as he said, both men fell into a hunched crouch, their olive-drab American uniforms melting into black with red bands around their arms. For one-hundredth of a second, she could have sworn she saw their fingertips stretch into claws.

But there wasn't time to stare. James was right behind her. As he pushed her forward, the air raid sirens went off. Loud and obnoxious, they wailed, going up and down, up and down as if to say no speed would be fast enough. No shelter would be safe. Eventually, these demons would catch them.

Garbled words made her look to James as they ran. He was trying to say something, but she couldn't hear him. And she didn't dare look back to see if they were being followed. But she didn't need to. She could feel it. In and out of airplanes he pulled her, holding her tightly to his side when he could, then pressing her forward again whenever the shiny black boots came too close.

Panting, they dove behind the gigantic wheel of a plane. "Where's your gun?" she rasped in ragged breaths.

"I don't know!" Before she could speak again, he'd grabbed her by the wrist and yanked her forward. She stumbled out of the way just as the taller Nazi plunged his knife into the tire she'd been leaning against.

For what seemed like an eternity, they continued the game of cat and mouse, running and hiding until the Nazis found them again. After a while, Clara began to feel like they were running in circles until she finally saw the warehouse James must have been pushing them toward. They stopped at the edge of a clearing between the warehouse and the field of planes.

"When I say go, run in a zig-zag pattern as fast as you can toward that door," James whispered in her ear. He pointed to a door in the side of the metal domed building. "Don't stop for me or anybody. And even if I'm not there, you go in without me. Understand?"

Clara wanted to tell him she wasn't going anywhere without

him, not again, but he didn't give her time to respond. Instead, he crouched on the other side of the plane until he waved her forward.

Clara knew better than to question him this time. Instead, she ran as fast as her shoes could carry her. Her speed wasn't impressive by any means, but James directed her with shouts as bullets whizzed past them and hit the metal building they were running toward.

"Go! Go! Go!" he called above the horrible symphony of bullets and sirens and the blood rushing in her ears.

Just as they reached the door, a bullet ricocheted. James cried out and grabbed his arm, but he managed to yank the door open anyway. He shoved her through before leaping in after her.

The metal door should have shut with a bang, and she expected the Nazis to jump through after them, as they hadn't had time to lock the door.

But the shouts never came, nor the sound of bullets. Instead, the warehouse was eerily quiet. She opened her eyes and willed herself to look around. And once again, they were somewhere new.

8

SUGAR PLUM WARNINGS

A sense of relief settled over her, but it was quickly choked out by exhaustion. How long could she go on like this without losing her sanity? On the cusp of death, they were whisked away to safety, only to be hunted again. And she'd only experienced it three times. James had made countless trips across the world. How many more could he survive?

Where was James? Clara sat up. The world around them was dark and chilly, and she sensed they were outside once again. She could just make out the hint of a purple light in the sky where the moon should have been, and she was rather sure she'd been lying with her head on his legs, sprawled out in whatever place of cold, wet darkness they had been sent to this time.

As if hearing her thoughts, James groaned. "I should have known." And though Clara couldn't see him, she imagined him running his hand through his short hair and leaning his head back, eyes closed the way he always did when he was angry or annoyed.

"What do you mean?" She kept her voice low in case the Nazis were nearby. Seeing the yellow eyes now before she was oriented might just give her a heart attack. "They looked real enough to me."

"That's not it." He pushed himself into a sitting position. "I should have known as soon as I saw them that it was too good to be true."

"I don't understand." She leaned over and tugged on his arm. "While you're thinking, let's at least get out of this cold." She glanced up at the dark purple sky. "Wherever we are."

And yet, James didn't move or speak. She shivered and crouched down beside him while she waited for him to answer. To her surprise and disappointment, he didn't put his arm around her.

How long they sat that way, she couldn't tell. While she waited, though, her eyes adjusted to the low light squeezing its way through the clouds. They were sitting on a wooden platform of some sort. Heaps of snow piled around the platform's railing and on the ground around them, but their spot, mercifully, looked to have been swept clean. She wanted to keep exploring, but the air was growing colder by the moment. She was losing feeling in her fingers so she tried again. Maybe if she coaxed him to answer, he would get up and figure out where they were.

"James, I—"

"Jones died in the jump at Normandy. Kelly lost a leg during a prior jump. They sent him back to the States several months before all... this started happening."

"Oh," she breathed, closing her eyes. "I'm so sorry."

He shrugged. "Guess I hoped it was a miracle. I got to see you after all. I figured... maybe I was getting them back, too." His shoulder drooped. "I've been doing this a long time, Clara. But something... something's not right. I missed the rats, and I shouldn't have. I would never have been caught off my guard like that before."

"James, you can't—"

"My focus is slipping. I'm trying to keep control, but I feel like it's starting to disintegrate." He groaned again and grabbed his right arm with his left hand.

"Your arm!" She remembered his cry from when they'd entered the metal building. She put her hand on his shoulders and used it to guide her as she scrambled over to his other side. "Is it bad?"

"No," he said, though she could tell he was grinding his teeth. "It only grazed me. I moved wrong just now, and it started throbbing. Here, help me up."

She reached out with both hands and found his chest by accident. And though she moved her hands to his arms as quickly as she could, she couldn't help marveling at how much harder his muscles were... everywhere. The darkness covered the hot blush rising from her neck. Now was not the time for such thoughts. She cleared her throat.

"Give me your hand," she said. His calloused hand found hers, and she helped him stand. By this time, large snowflakes were beginning to fall. As they stood, she finally realized they were standing on the back porch of a little house. The house was made of brick and had a little yellow door just feet from where they had awakened.

"Where are we this time?" she asked.

"I haven't been here in a long time," he said softly, his injured arm seemingly forgotten. He walked to the door, hesitating just for a second before reaching out and pulling it open.

As soon as they were inside, James turned and locked the door behind them. "I told them to keep this locked," he muttered to himself, shaking his head.

Clara gave him a curious look, but he didn't answer. Instead, he looked around with an obvious satisfaction at what appeared to be a little kitchen. His shoulders relaxed for the first time since they'd been reunited.

Clara turned and studied their surroundings as well. What was here that made him so relaxed? And who were the people he'd warned to lock the door?

There weren't any lights on in the kitchen, but enough light spilled in from the next room over that Clara could see. The kitchen was small, much smaller than her parents' at home, but large enough to fit a round wooden table with space enough for four seats, though there were eight squeezed around it. A black cast-iron stove stood in the corner, still radiating heat. Pretty yellow curtains hung on the little window above the sink, though the black window coverings somewhat ruined the tranquility they might have provided. Three wooden shelves also painted yellow stood out from the yellow rose wallpaper and held an assortment of teacups, spices, baking soda, and canisters labeled, Coffee, Sugar, and Flour. A little bit of bread had been left on one of the plates, but it was an unappetizing shade of gray. Crumbles of cheese sat on another plate, and what appeared to be the remnants of thin brown soup covered the bottom of a bowl. Most of the dishes were scraped clean. Sounds came from the next room. Unlike those in the pub, however, these sounds were sweet and full of innocent delight.

James was already heading for the next room, so she followed. In the low light, she spotted the tear in his sleeve. Thankfully, it hadn't bled as badly as she'd feared.

"I take it you like this place?" she whispered as she followed him.

"This is my favorite place in all of Europe," he said quietly, a small smile on his lips. As they passed the table, he stopped her and picked up a glass. He handed it to her. "Smell it," he said, a tired ghost of mischief in his eye. "What do you think it is?"

Clara did as she was told. And to her surprise, the scent was familiar. "Coca-Cola!" She stared at the glass in wonder. "How did you get that all the way over here?"

"General Eisenhower thought we needed it." James grinned more genuinely this time. "For morale. Some of the troops down south even have their own bottling plants and everything."

"Is that where this came from?"

"I don't know. All I know is that it's nice to have a taste of home sometimes, and the Brits over here just can't get enough."

"Is that where we are? Still in Britain?"

He took her hand and led her to stand in the doorway of the next room. "We sure are."

As little as Clara had liked the chaos of the pub, this new scene was enchanting. A thin woman in a faded blue sweater played merrily on an old piano, looking behind her and laughing as she did. Four children, looking between the ages of two and twelve, were dancing in circles around the small living room between the piano and the little Christmas tree by the window. The tree was simple but sweet, covered in tinsel and handmade ornaments. Two men in American uniforms stood beside the piano, singing the carols as the woman played, and teasing the children.

"Who are they?" Clara asked as she gazed at the cozy little scene.

"The Taylors. Mary Taylor," James pointed to the woman, "hasn't seen her husband in several years. See those thick curtains?" He pointed at the windows, which were covered completely by curtains and were far too large for the little room. "Those keep most of the light out in case the German bombers decide to make a flyover."

"In case of an air raid," Clara breathed. She'd never experienced an actual air raid, but the practice drills in Eagle's Head had been frightening enough. Her heart went out to the poor mother, having to live here in the middle of a war zone with her four babies.

James nodded, his face more serious as he looked back down at the children. "The GIs were asked to spend Christmas with whatever family invited us. It helps, to quote my commander, '-to fill the empty seats left by the British fighting men.'" Then he smiled a little. "The families also appreciate all the extra rations the Americans are given, things that are hard to get here like soap and chocolate." His grin widened. "And Coca-Cola."

"The GIs don't seem to mind," Clara said as she watched the two soldiers playing with the children.

James shook his head. "Those are two of my friends, Feinwick and Owens."

Clara gave him a skeptical look. "They're still alive, aren't they?"

"Last I saw, they were just as alive as ever."

That made Clara feel slightly better. Maybe these friends wouldn't turn out to be Nazis, too.

"Anyway," James continued, his eyes back on the children, "we all thought it was nice being invited here. We don't mind sharing, and they more than give back with making us feel a little more human again."

She studied his face carefully. "As opposed to?"

But instead of answering, he darted forward and grabbed the second tallest girl by the hand and pulled her back over to Clara.

"Clara, I would like you to meet my dance instructor, Ann."

Clara couldn't help laughing. She had no reason to be jealous after all. "Well, hello, Ann. It's nice to meet you."

Ann grinned back. "And you."

She looked to be about ten years old with an adorable sprinkling of freckles on her nose and luminous brown eyes. A little too skinny perhaps, but her smile was infectious and her eyes were kind.

"I call her the sugar plum fairy," James said, trying to poke her as she laughed and dodged his hand. "The first time we were here, she ate the whole bag of candy my sister had sent."

"You said I could have some," Ann returned his grin with an even feistier one. "You never said how much!"

James rolled his eyes and smiled. "Then the least you can do is give me a dance." He bowed to Ann, who giggled and took his hand. She led him to the center of the room, her brown curls bouncing.

As she watched them, smiling and laughing, Clara's eyes pricked. She tried blinking the discomfort away. But by the time she'd pasted a smile back on her face, James had excused himself from his little jig with Ann. His brows were furrowed as he took Clara's hand.

"What's wrong?" He looked up and down her body as though searching for a visible injury.

Clara shook her head. But when she tried to speak, her voice betrayed her.

"I just thought...." She took a deep breath and cleared her throat. "You're so good with children, and I'd never dreamed the war would go on so long, and now—"

"James."

They looked down to find Ann staring expectantly up at him. Clara tried to wipe her tears on her shoulder before the girl could see.

"One of the floorboards in the hall has a hole in it," Ann continued. "And we think a mouse is coming up through it at night. Do you think you could look at it? Mother said we could ask you."

James gave Clara one more long look before nodding and heading down to the hall. Before she could ask the little girl about Christmas presents, school, or some other lame topic, Ann took her by the hand and led her back into the kitchen. Without asking, she sat Clara in a chair before seating herself on a tall stool by the sink.

"You don't have much time," she said in a low voice. "You'll have to make your decision soon."

Clara gaped at the girl. They didn't have much time. She'd heard that before. But it was a minute before she recalled those same words from Godfather Drosselmeyer.

"My decision? About what?" How did this little girl know about James's plight? Was she a Nazi in disguise, too? "This is a dream," she added, almost belligerently. "I'm just trying to help him so I can finish the dream." Why was she even talking about this? With a dream child from her dream world, no less.

"You can't save him." Ann shook her head matter-of-factly, which only annoyed Clara more.

"I know that," Clara said, shifting in her seat. "It's just a dream after all."

"Then why are you trying so hard if it's just a dream?"

Clara huffed and changed the subject. "What do you mean I can't save him?"

"You've been here long enough. It should be obvious."

Clara stared at her, unable to even come up with a semi-coherent answer.

The girl sighed and tilted her head with more than a bit of condescension. "What has he told you?"

Clara paused. How much should she tell this girl? Was she just another figment of Clara's imagination, bent on keeping her from having her happy ending with James? Or did Ann truly know something Clara did not?

It was a dream after all. What did she have to lose but her heart?

"He doesn't know how long he's been running or how he

became involved with the Nazis," she finally said. "He just knows that wherever he goes, they're there as well. And his job is to stop them." She shuddered and was suddenly quite grateful the windows in this house were all covered.

Ann sighed and muttered something to herself as she hopped off the stool. In stocking feet, she crossed the kitchen and grabbed a plate of sliced brown cake covered in a glaze. She held it out to Clara and gestured for her to take one. When Clara had, she took one as well and settled back up on the stool. "Pay attention. I have a lot to tell you and not much time."

Clara couldn't have looked away if she'd tried.

"Sergeant James Parker doesn't know what day it is or why he moves. He simply moves. Every few days. Never longer than a week." She paused, cake halfway to her mouth. "That's why he doesn't know the war is over. Nor does he remember that he's been moved two hundred and thirty-seven times since Normandy."

Well, that wasn't helpful at all. If anything, it only made the situation seem more muddled than before.

"But," Ann said, as if expecting skepticism, "the rats are closing in. That's why you're here. You have a decision to make soon, and you don't have long to make it. And before you ask how they've moved so far over the map, that's just the way of the rats. No matter where he goes, they do too." She paused, and looked down at the cake in her hands. "As they will for the rest of his life."

"No." Clara stood up from her chair. "They won't." She narrowed her eyes at the black covering on the window. "I won't let them."

Ann arched an eyebrow. "And how, precisely, do you plan to stop them?"

Clara searched for an answer, but none came to mind.

Ann, looking very cheeky for such a young girl, rolled her eyes. "Sit back down. I'm not done."

Clara obeyed, but she glared to make her displeasure clear. "Why doesn't he go to anyone for help?"

"You forget. With the exception of you, no one else can see the rats."

There it was again. Even Ann called the Nazis rats. Why? "But you—"

"This is not about me. This is about you and him." Ann took one last bite of cake and brushed the crumbs off her dress. "As to getting help, he finally learned after being thrown into the psychiatric ward enough times that no one believes him."

Clara froze. "They thought he was insane?"

Ann shrugged. "Wouldn't you if someone came to you and said Nazi-rats were chasing them? And when they pointed, no one was there?"

That question made Clara more than a little uncomfortable for more reasons than one. "Then why doesn't he just stay near people, since they don't go into crowded areas?"

"That would be fine," Ann said, "if it were possible to stay in a crowded area forever. But dream or not, James needs food and sleep, and it's hard to get those in crowded market squares, especially if you don't have any money."

Only then did it occur to Clara that they'd forgotten to pay the barkeep at the pub for their beer. And the barkeep hadn't cared. "Then how did he survive this long?" She tried to do the math in her head. How many meals would he have needed in the last year and a half?

"People try to help. Around here, anyway. But there's not much to go around for us, either. And if he wasn't an injured American, it would be even less." For the first time, Ann cast a longing glance back at the next room, looking very much like a little girl again. "We don't have much here to give," she said in a quiet voice. "The Germans have done their best to cut us off from everyone. Not that it matters." She closed her eyes for a moment before opening them and shaking her head. "Either way, he barely gets enough time to catch his breath before they come after him again."

Clara searched for words as she fingered the buttons on her dress. "I don't understand any of this," she finally said. "But you seem to. Why?" She stood and stared at the faded roses on the wallpaper. "Why is this the most realistic dream I've ever had? Dreams can't be real. None of this is real."

Ann tilted her head and tapped her finger on her chin. "And yet, here you are. Arguing with an imaginary nine-year-old."

Clara had nothing she could say to that. So instead, she asked the question she'd been pondering since she realized it was a dream. "So why am I here? Why would everything change now?" Notwithstanding that it was all a foolish dream.

Ann stood directly in front of her, her eyes wide as she stared up at Clara. "I told you," she said evenly, her thin face solemn. "He doesn't have much time. He may seem like himself for now. But you're losing him fast. And before you do, you'll have to make that choice."

Clara tensed. "What choice?"

"You need to accept that you'll never be able to chase the rats away. Not completely, at least. That's just life, and you have no choice in the matter." She took a step closer. "But the time will come soon when you need to decide whether you can share James with them or not. If you can live like this for the rest of your life."

Clara's blood ran cold. "No." She shook her head vehemently. "I won't." She reflected on all the time they'd spent together since he'd arrived at her house. "He's going to be fine. He's doing better now than he did when I first saw him even!" But as she spoke, she remembered the way he'd admitted his confusion out on the porch. How his control was slipping.

"I know it seems that way," Ann said softly, putting a small hand on Clara's knee. "And he might even make improvements. But he's never going to be the same man you sent off to war. They'll always be there, hiding underneath." She gave Clara a sad smile. "The rats will never go away."

Clara folded her arms belligerently. "I don't believe that."

Ann looked genuinely surprised. And somewhat disappointed. "So if you're wrong, then you're just going to leave him?"

"No." Clara took a step toward the door, but Ann grabbed her arm.

"What do you mean then?"

"I mean," Clara hissed, "that I refuse to make that decision because I'm not going to let them have him."

"That's not a good idea," Ann began, but Clara pulled her wrist free. James might not be able to end this. But she would. Before she went to find James, however, she paused in the doorway and turned back.

"Who are you?" She studied the girl, looking for something, anything that might reveal her secrets. "And how do you know all this?"

Ann tilted her head and gave her a small, nearly fierce smile. "You said a prayer and made a wish, didn't you?"

Clara nodded. She'd prayed and wished for him to come home more times than she could count. A lot of good it did me, she nearly said aloud as she made her way down the hall to find James.

He was kneeling in the middle of the hall with tools spread around him. Her heart hurt a bit as she imagined him in their future home—the one that almost was—puttering around and fixing things like this for the rest of his days.

He pulled a nail from between his lips. "I don't know why they asked me to do this. I don't know the first thing about floors. But this should at least keep the critters out. There." He pointed to a pile of nails near her feet. "Would you hand me another one of those?"

Clara couldn't answer, but she did as he asked. All she could think about was the girl's question. Why was she trying so hard to save him?

At first, the answer had been obvious. She couldn't bear to see him hurt, even in a dream. But now…. Did she actually think she might stand a chance at bringing him home? Was that why she was trying so hard to make sense of this mad charade? And Ann seemed to think Clara was making a bad choice by trying to stop the rats. What did she think would happen if Clara disobeyed?

"Well," he said, standing, "I'm going to go back in to watch the kids open presents." He grinned at her, all signs of alarm or even general suspicion gone from his face. "Aren't you coming?"

It was strange. He hadn't even mentioned the rats once since entering the house. She followed him back to the happy little room, where he picked up a conversation with his friends, acting as though he hadn't a care in the world.

At first, this dream had begun as a gift from Heaven, strange as it was. But now it was turning into a nightmare. Everything had spiraled out of her control, and she was too emotionally vested. She needed to wake up. Caring this deeply was beyond healthy. It had to be.

And yet… was there a chance Ann was right? Could the decisions she made here somehow touch the real world?

As Clara sat waffling, one of the little boys tripped and fell into a curtain, knocking it away from the window just enough for Clara to make out the pair of beady yellow eyes through the window pane. They were trained on her.

Though fear made her tremble, those eyes also lit a flame in her belly, and she was walking across the room to James. Her decision was made.

"James," she whispered to him, plastering a smile on her face for his friends, "I need to talk to you."

He gave her a grin and reached around to elbow her playfully. "About what?"

She scowled and slapped his arm away. "Would you stop that?" She lowered her voice so as not to alarm the children. "They're here," she whispered, giving the window a pointed glance. "The rats. They're outside that window."

Instead of looking concerned, or going to the window to check it out, however, he just ruffled her hair. "Aw, Clara, you can't let a few rodents ruin your evening." Then he turned to his friends and took another swig of Coca-Cola. "She hates rats," he chuckled. "When we were in fifth grade...."

As he told the story to his friends, Clara felt the weight of someone's gaze. Sure enough, when she turned around, Ann was watching her, warning, even pleading with her eyes. But Clara just looked away and deliberately placed her foot behind his. Then she took a step and stumbled dramatically.

"You okay?" James bent down to help her, but she waved him off.

"I'm fine. Just give me a second to find my...." She pretended to search for something on the floor. As soon as he had turned back to his conversation, she tucked her hand beneath his trouser leg and slipped out his knife. He moved his leg, and she froze, sure he'd seen her. But when he kept talking and nothing happened, she stood and dashed toward the back door. She didn't know how, but she was going to end this.

The snow was still falling when she stepped out into the cold and closed the door behind her. The air was soft and tranquil, the kind of silence that could be heard. She paused on the threshold, every muscle in her body begging her to go back inside, trying to seize up as fear threatened to take over her senses. She gripped the knife so hard her fingers nearly lost feeling.

What was she doing out here anyway? She didn't have any military training. She knew not to tuck her thumb into her fist when throwing a punch. But that was only because James had taught her better in fourth grade after she'd tried to punch him for hiding her favorite doll in a tree. She missed, and he laughed so hard he'd fallen over before showing her how to hit someone "properly," as he put it.

"If you leave your thumb in," he said as he rearranged her hand, "you're gonna break your fingers. Then you'll have missed and you'll have no way to hit them back."

Clara hadn't gotten into any more fights after that, particularly after a passerby had tattled to her mother. And though she was taller and stronger now than she'd been back then, she didn't know any more what to do with the knife than she would have in fourth grade. And yet... she had to do something.

Against her foot's will, she forced it to take a step toward the side of the house where she'd seen the Nazi. Then the other. Then the right again. Like a stiff wind-up toy, she made her way into the deeper shadows of the night. Every hair on her body stood on end. Would they kill her silently while she tried to stalk them? A trained killer would have no more difficulty taking her down than Edward would breaking the neck of one of his farm chickens for supper.

She tried to tread as silently as her shoes would allow, then came to a stop at the edge of the snowdrift on the right side of the house. These Nazis, whoever they were, liked to play. If they'd wanted to kill James and her, they would have done so a long time ago. Perhaps she could play off that ego. And maybe she could even take a few down before they realized what she was doing. Letting out another frosty breath, she walked again to the window where she'd seen the eyes.

"I... I'm here!" Her first words were so faint she barely heard them herself. She licked her dry lips and tried again. "You've been trying to get him. I want to save him." She swallowed. "So it appears we're at an impasse." Could she sound any more vulnerable?

For a long time, there was no response. Snowflakes continued to drift from the deep purple sky as the moon tried unsuccessfully to peek through the clouds. She was about to go back inside when the snow crunched. She had to stifle a shriek as a black shape emerged from the hedge. She could see the contours of his boots and uniform, but out of the corner of her eye, she could have sworn something flicked back and forth behind him. His yellow eyes stood out even in the heavy dark, and for one split second, she was sure she could see the flash of razor-sharp teeth. Her breathing sped, and she had to bite her lip to keep from screaming. What kind of enemy had James gotten himself caught up with?

"You are braver than we expected," said a raspy voice in a thick German accent. "I like this one, no?" he chuckled, as though making a joke. How many of them were there? She nearly fainted when his hot breath was suddenly on the back of her neck. "So you want to talk?"

Clara nodded and swallowed again, willing her voice to be strong. "I want to know why you're keeping him here."

"Oh, we're not keeping him anywhere!" The raspy voice laughed, moving this time to her left. He was circling her. "He can leave anytime he wants."

She squeezed the handle of the knife. "That's not what he says," she spat back. "He says you chase him everywhere. And from what I've seen tonight, he's telling the truth."

"And let me guess. That little girl in there told you there is no hope. Am I right?"

Clara stiffened. They knew about Ann, too? She cleared her throat. "Just answer the question."

"So I am right." A smile crept through his voice. "And yet, here are you." He moved closer. "Why?"

"I have to try," Clara whispered.

"Of course you do." He paused, and when he spoke again, his voice was far too cheery. "I respect bravery in any form. So how about this? I will make you a deal."

The heat from his body warmed her as he moved to stand in front of her again.

"You answer my riddle, and I will tell you how to save him."

She frowned. "A riddle?"

"You seem like a smart girl. Solve the riddle, and I will tell you how to get your beloved soldier home."

This was a trick. It had to be. Maybe she should stab whatever he... it was then and there. But the more she talked with him, the more she realized there was even more to this strange world than she'd first thought. If she could only keep him talking a few minutes longer....

"Fine," she snapped. "Give me the riddle."

"Very well." She could hear his leer in every word. How she wished she could slap that smile off his horrid face. But she forced her hands to stay at her sides as she listened.

"What can smother, blind, and bury, but cannot be slashed, blocked, or held?"

"What?"

"I told you, what can smother, blind, and bury? But it can't be slashed, blocked, or held?"

Her hopes had been paper thin to start with, but now they went up in flames as she racked her brain for anything that might work. A blanket could smother, blind, and be used in a burial, but it could be slashed.

"Smoke?" she guessed.

They burst into laughter.

An arm wrapped itself around her waist, and a whimper slipped from Clara's throat as claws cut through the Nazi's leather gloves and then through her dress. A human mouth brushed her cheek, its breath on her face. But as it did, something else brushed her neck as well. Were those... whiskers?

She willed herself to remain still, though she wanted nothing more than to yank out the knife and stab him… it… in the heart. But she held steady and did her best to answer. She just needed them to tell her a little more. Just a little more. For James's sake.

"Smoke cannot bury," the voice sneered. "Try again."

"Fire?" she asked breathlessly.

"No."

"Sand?"

"Try again." Two, maybe three sets of laughter joined the first again. She could hear the crunch of their boots in the snow as they surrounded her.

Try as she might, though, Clara couldn't come up with any more answers. Maybe, during the day in a quiet room without a whiskered, yellow-eyed villain holding her close, she could have. But not here as she fought for James's life.

"See?" the voice said. "This is why your knife won't work here."

Clara closed her eyes and bit her lip. They knew about the knife. She was toast.

"It's also why your soldier is dying." It finally let go of her waist and stepped away. It no longer sounded amused, and Clara got the feeling that its patience was coming to an end. "Your soldier is drowning. And it seems as though you just don't want to save him."

Clara screamed and plunged her knife into the place where the Nazi's heart should have been. But the blade bit air, not flesh, and the sense of other beings nearby was gone. She was alone. But there wasn't a moment to lose.

"James!" she screamed, running back to the porch. Her hands shook so badly she could barely open the door. But when she finally heard the latch click and was able to swing the door wide open, she was not in the kitchen, but in the last place she'd expected.

9

NOT LIKE YOU

The wind whistled across the baseball field and sent a chill through Clara's dress. She squinted against the reflection of the moon on the snow. The field looked empty, just as it should on Christmas night. But just before she panicked, she spotted him in the dugout, staring out at the field.

The urgency of her task ahead warred with longing as she carefully walked across the thinnest spots of snow to reach him. Out here, the Nazis seemed a dream of their own... or a nightmare, rather. Here on this field, it only felt like Clara and James, the same way they had always been. She only had to close her eyes and inhale deeply, and she was back in high school, listening to him spin tales about how the world was theirs. All they had to do was get married and take it.

When she drew close, he patted the bench next to him. She nearly died of bliss when she was able to cuddle up against him, and he removed his coat, wrapping it around her shoulders and pulling her close.

"What were you doing with this?" He took the knife from her hand, looking confused.

She bit her lip. "Nothing, apparently."

He chuckled and put the knife back in its case. Then he leaned back and wrapped an arm around her shoulders. "I missed this," he said. "I can't tell you how many nights I went to sleep pretending we were here."

Clara stroked his arm. "I've missed it, too." She needed to get up. They needed to get up and go. Where they were going, she hadn't the slightest idea, but she knew they'd better figure out the Nazi's riddle, and they'd better do it fast.

And yet, as she tucked her head into his neck, just below his jaw, the warmth of his skin on her face with the cold air enveloping them, she never wanted to move again. If they could stay in this moment forever, she would be perfectly satisfied.

But it wasn't to be.

"James," she said softly, hating herself for breaking the moment's perfection. "We need to talk—"

"I saw you crying in there."

She blinked at him. "What?"

"Back in the cottage." He turned and looked down at her, his blue eyes gentle as he traced the shape of her face with the backs of his fingers.

"But this can't wait," she said, shaking her head. "It's important. We—"

"So is this."

As he continued to trace the contours of her face, Clara very nearly forgot what she was supposed to say. His fingertips were cool. They generally were, but not in an unpleasant way. She gave a shaky sigh and closed her eyes as they trailed from her temple down to her lips.

"You were sad," he said. "Why?"

With all the excitement over the Nazis, Clara had nearly forgotten. But as soon as he brought it up, the familiar pain tightened in her chest.

He was quiet for a minute. Then he whispered, "Was it the children?"

A strange half-sob escaped from her chest. What was wrong with her? She needed to get herself together. They didn't have time for this! And yet, tears streamed down her face as though she'd never cried before.

Gathering her in his arms, he pulled her onto his lap and whispered, "I thought we'd have a family by now, too."

Unable to speak, Clara simply nodded. His calloused thumbs gently rubbed her back as she cried into his chest. And though she knew he wouldn't have admitted it for the world, she felt his chest tighten as well.

Which only made her cry harder.

After shedding what felt like every last tear in her body, she leaned back and gave a shaky sigh and dried her face on his sleeve. "Usually I'm the one scoffing at people who cry easily, but tonight I've cried more than I have in my entire life."

"I have an idea," he said, wrapping the coat around her more tightly. His eyes still had dark circles beneath them, but there was a glimmer in them that she hadn't seen since…. Well, since he'd left.

"But we need to talk." She took a deep breath and tried to look as serious as the situation called for, rather than weepy and tired the way she felt.

"How about this? Hear me out, and we'll talk about whatever you want for the rest of the night."

Clara shook her head. "James—"

"Look," he took her free hand in his and squeezed it, the light leaving his eyes again as he stared out at the field. "I don't have much time left. I don't know how I know it, but… I know." He swallowed and looked down at her again. "Just give me this? Please? For five minutes. We can afford five minutes."

She wanted so badly to argue. They needed to figure out the

riddle. But the look he was giving her nearly shattered her already broken heart. How could she deny him this when in all likelihood, she was about to lose him forever?

"Okay," she whispered. "Five minutes. What do you want to talk about?"

His face broke into a wide, crooked grin, and he snuggled closer, looking rather pleased with himself. His joy made her heart thump unevenly. "Let's make up a family," he said.

Clara let out a somewhat delirious laugh. "What? Right now?"

"Right now! We've got nothing to lose!"

Again, that warning voice in her head advised against such an activity. Losing him when she woke up was going to be hard enough. Now she was going to lose their imaginary children as well?

Still, before the warning was even complete, Clara told that voice to kindly shut up. She'd already come this far. If she was destined for heartache, which it seemed she was, then that heartache was going to be worth it.

"Fine then." She folded her hands on her lap and looked at him expectantly. "Shall we start with a boy or a girl?"

"Hm." He studied the field as though he could see it filled with children now. "I always thought triplets would be an adventure."

She pulled away to glower at him.

"Or," he said, chuckling, "a boy would be fun, but a girl might be sweet."

Clara nudged him and laughed. "If he's anything like you, I'll need three girls to be properly prepared for him."

James exploded in laughter. "You were no little angel yourself!"

"I was, too!"

"You hit me with a baseball! In the head!"

"That was an accident!" She slapped him on the leg.

"See?" He deflected her slap and pinned her arms to her sides. "So much violence!"

She laughed, loud and long like she hadn't in a long time. And it felt even better when he joined her. Soon they both had tears running down their faces as they struggled to catch their breath. Guilt smoldered at the edge of her joy, but Clara tried to bat it away. What if James was right and his time was running out? Shouldn't they make the most out of what they had here and now? Just for a few moments?

He put his hand on her knee, after their laughter had died away. "I've been thinking about something."

She leaned her head against his shoulder and closed her eyes. "And what would that be?"

"I know I always wanted to make a career out of the army." He took a deep breath. "But I think... I think I'd like to do something else instead." He looked around. "You know, in case by some miracle we ever escape this madness."

Clara sat up. "Are you going to join your father's business?"

He shook his head. "Nah. I'd travel even more with him than I would in the army." He looked at her, his clear eyes wide. "I was actually thinking... maybe I'd like to teach math. Like Mr. Jacobson."

"That's definitely a change," she said. "And I'd love to have you home, but why now?"

James reached under the bench and picked up a forgotten ball. He tossed it and caught it again. "I want to be there for you. And our kids."

"Do you regret your time in the army?"

"No. It needed to be done, and someone had to do it. I just... I think that someone isn't me anymore. I've seen too much. It's time for somebody else."

Snow began to fall again, and Clara was jarred out of her

bubble of peace. The Nazis were nowhere to be seen, but that could change at any minute. And so could James's fate.

"James," she said softly. "I hate to say this, but we need to—"

"I wish we'd eloped." He cleared his throat and squeezed the ball until his hand shook. "I wish we hadn't listened to them and had just gotten married anyway." His shoulders drooped slightly. "We might have even have a kid by now."

"A child that would have lived his early life entirely without his father," Clara said gently, putting her hands on his arms. She extricated herself from his arms and moved to sit beside him on the bench. "But I mean it. You said if we talked about what you wanted, you would help me figure out how to end all this."

"What about Edward?" he asked, studying the baseball. "Did he ever find a girl?"

Clara stiffened. For a little while, she'd been able to forget their friend's strange proposal, but now that part of her evening flooded back with excruciating clarity.

"He doesn't have a girlfriend," she said as lightly as she could manage. "He's doing well, though. His father plans to turn over the farm soon, I think."

But he knew her too well to be fooled. Getting off the bench, he knelt in front of her.

"What aren't you telling me?"

"It's nothing."

"Clara, something is bothering you. What is it?" He paused. "Is it Edward?" His eyes narrowed. "Did he do anything he shouldn't have?"

"No, he didn't do anything."

"Well, judging by the look on your face, he did." Then his mouth fell open, and his eyes widened. "Wait, you're not... seeing him. Are you?"

"No! I mean, he asked me. But I haven't actually answered him."

James fell back on his heels, shock on his face, and Clara wanted to kick herself for even hinting at Edward's suggestion. Kicking Edward wouldn't have been too bad, either, for putting her in this position.

"But you're thinking about it," James whispered. His eyes hardened like ice as he fell back a step. "You broke your promise!"

"James, you've been missing for a year and a half!" Clara exploded. "And my heart has not wavered once in my love for you. But what do you expect me to do? Hm? When everyone came home except for you, I held out hope. And I've continued to hold out! But how long am I supposed to wait?" She was crying now as she spoke, and he was walking in circles, his hands on the back of his head.

"Of all the backstabbing traitors to walk the earth...." He glared at her. "And you're just as bad. If not worse!"

"Then when were you planning to come home?" she cried. "In a month? Five years? Ten? Never? Look, I don't want to marry him or anybody else but you! Can you blame me, though, for wondering about the future? Wondering what happens if you never come home?"

"I've been trying!" he shouted. "I have been trying the best that I know how to get back to you. But I don't know how!" He began to turn away, then whirled back around and jabbed a finger at her. "And yes, I have every right to be angry! You made a promise, as did I. I've been faithful, Clara! Not once did I even consider loving anyone else but you!"

"What is wrong with you!"

"What's wrong with *me*?" he echoed incredulously.

"This isn't like you!" As she uttered the words, she remembered Ann's warning, the one she'd so flippantly shrugged off. He was getting better, Clara stubbornly insisted. And for the first part of their conversation on the bench, he's seemed more himself than ever. But now…. He had always been protective, but never jealous. Not like this. And the knowledge that Ann was right only fired her anger. Clara threw her hands up. "You know what? I knew this was a mistake."

"What?" he snapped. "Agreeing to marry me?"

"Letting this charade continue!" she screamed back. "I knew from the beginning that letting myself get involved in this crazy dream was idiotic. You're not real!" She gestured wildly to the world around them. "None of this is real! And now I'm going to always think of our last time together as this!" She grabbed the forgotten baseball and threw it at the fence as hard as she could, relishing in its satisfying clang. "And it's nothing more than a stupid dream!"

He wrapped a hand around her shoulder and tried to pull her toward him. "Clara!"

"Go away." She batted his hand away. She needed to wake up. All she had to do was wake up, and this insanity would be over. There wouldn't be any heroics this night, nor would there be a happily ever after. But at least she could try to forget his look of betrayal that would haunt her forever.

But before she could walk away, he yanked her into his chest and threw her to the ground. She opened her eyes just in time to hear a metallic screech and to see him throw his body over hers. Clara screamed. They were still in a field, but not the one she expected. The baseball field with its soft layer of white snow was gone. This field was new. And it was covered in machinery, men, and flames.

10

DARK

*S*houts rang out around them, but Clara couldn't tell who was fighting whom. Tanks recoiled as they fired into the air, and the tattering of machine guns made individual sounds impossible to locate. Flames danced on top of vehicles and trees, and black smoke billowed high in the sky. Between the sounds and the heat and the blinding light from the flames, she just wanted to put her head down and hide. But they couldn't stay here.

"James!" She had to shout over the explosions as he pressed down on her. "What do we do?" She was more than grateful for his protection, but the longer they lay there, the heavier he became.

But James didn't answer. He just pulled his arms up to his face, forcing Clara to bend her neck and press her ear against her shoulder. Though the new position wasn't comfortable, she could now see that they were on a bridge that ran over a brook separating the two fields, though she still couldn't tell which side belonged to which country. They were also, much to her relief, very near the edge of the battle. If they climbed off the bridge into the water, perhaps they could follow the brook into the darkness. Anything to get away from here.

"James!" she yelled again. "What do we do?"

But he didn't respond. She tried to crane her neck around to see if he was alright, fear hammering in her chest. Had he been hit? She couldn't see him well enough to know. Behind the fear came regret. They shouldn't have stayed at the baseball field talking. She'd known the consequences of failing to solve the riddle, and now he was going to pay for it. Was this where the Nazis meant him to end?

A movement caught her eye. Her heart caught in her throat when she recognized the familiar black boots standing on the other side of the bridge. But for the first time, the Nazi's face was perfectly lit by the flames erupting around them.

Clara screamed.

The face had been human. At one time. But now, beady, yellow eyes glowed as they stared back at her. The Nazi no longer stood tall but hunched, and the tail Clara thought she'd imagined earlier flicked menacingly behind him. Patches of fur covered what had been skin. And when she was so horrified that she could no longer look away, its lips curled back into a smile, revealing two rows of needle-like teeth. It reached into its pocket and pulled something out. But Clara couldn't tell what it was until the rat pulled the pin and held it in the air.

"James!" Clara shrieked. She rolled out from beneath him and was on her feet in an instant. James, however, didn't move. She whirled around to grab him and drag him to the brook, but as she did, he curled up, knees against his chest as he covered his ears with his hands. His tears shone in the light of the flames.

Clara looked back up at the Nazi. His terrible grin spread from ear to ear as he tossed the grenade into the air.

"James!" Clara whispered. But no matter how hard she

pulled or pushed, he didn't move. It was all she could do to wrap her arms around him and close her eyes.

"Please," she prayed silently, "don't let it hurt too much."

But the expected blow never came. When she finally had the courage to look up, the noise ceased. Gone were the bombs, flames, and the stench of death and burning metal. They were still on the bridge, and the brook still bubbled beneath them. Instead of being surrounded by war, however, the scene was peaceful. A sugary snow was dusting the green fields that rose up on each side of the bridge. Two lampposts wrapped in homemade garlands illuminated the flakes as they fell all around her. A farmhouse glowed warm in the distance, its windows golden with light. It should have been lovely, except for the sound of James's quiet sobbing.

Clara took his face in her hands. "James," she said softly. "It's over. The battle's done."

But James only got on his knees and wrapped his arms around his head, squeezing his eyes shut even tighter as tears continued to roll down his face. "It's not gone," he whimpered. "It's always here!"

"What's here?" Clara looked around for signs of the Nazis, but they were gone, too.

"The darkness," he choked. "It's suffocating. And it never leaves!" His voice rose in pitch and volume until he was shouting. "It never leaves! And I can't take it anymore! I just can't take it!"

Clara stood, unsure of what to do. She looked around for someone who might help. Maybe the farmer from the distant house might be outside to hear her. But just as she was about to beg James to walk with her to the house, it struck her.

Darkness. The answer to the riddle was darkness.

What can smother, blind, and bury, but can't be slashed, blocked, or held?

James was being smothered by the darkness. It had blinded him to the truth of their situations, and it was burying him alive. But unlike an evil she could come at with weapons, this enemy couldn't be rivaled by strength. That was why she hadn't been able to kill the rat with the knife. It was why James struggled with the same enemies time and time again. No matter how many opponents he beat in his lifetime, he couldn't overpower this one. Neither of them could.

The rats had lied. Ann had been right.

All remaining hope drained from Clara's body and soul as she fell to her knees beside him. All this time they'd spent running, and it was all for naught. The darkness was there in his head, and that was where the battle raged. That's why the chase never stopped.

Though it felt like a century ago, Clara recalled Mrs. McCarty's words from earlier that afternoon in the shop. At the time, they'd seemed cold and crass. But maybe... just maybe she could understand a little more where the woman was coming from.

All I can say, Clara, is that you should consider yourself lucky James never made it home. At least you can move on with your life and start with someone new. It looks like I'll be stuck with my husband now until one of us dies of old age or madness.

Clara didn't want to move on. She wanted James. But even if they somehow recovered the life they'd planned and prayed about for years, she had the feeling it would never be the same. There would always be darkness that not even she could chase away. No matter how many smiles and touches she shared, they would never be enough to erase the sensations that must be burned into his mind. Maybe there had been a chance earlier, perhaps if she'd found him sooner, maybe she could have kept him in the light.

Not that it mattered now, though. She was too late. The

smart, self-assured, affectionate man she'd leaned on her entire life was falling to pieces in front of her. She watched now as he begged and pleaded for God to make it stop.

And she didn't know what to do.

At one point, she would have given anything for just another minute with him. But now, the pain on his face and the fear in his soft moans was growing to be more than she could bear. How could Clara expect to give him her entire life if she couldn't bear to look at him for another hour or even another five minutes? But she couldn't just leave him here. Dream or not, she couldn't abandon him to suffer for the rest of his days. And yet, if she was honest with herself, she wanted nothing more than to wake up and leave it all behind.

So this was what Ann had meant.

"Please, God," she whispered, turning away to shut out the image of him shaking on the ground. "I don't know what to do."

"Clara?"

Clara had been staring down into the inky water flowing beneath the bridge, but she jerked up at the sound of her name. At first, she thought it was James. But when she looked back, he was still huddled on the ground, his arms still wrapped around his head.

"Clara!" It wasn't James's voice at all. Instead, it belonged to—

Clara bolted upright in bed. The light blinded her as she gasped for air. The bridge and fields were gone, and so was the night. Instead, a fresh layer of newly fallen snow covered the street outside, the sun's reflection making it nearly blinding. Fritz watched her with wide eyes, his hand still outstretched from when he'd reached out to shake her awake.

"Clara," he whispered, "are you alright?"

Clara couldn't answer. She was too busy searching every corner and shadow of her bedroom. But James was gone.

11

THE LAST

"**A**re you okay?" Fritz asked again, his eyes the size of golf balls.

Clara was tempted not to answer. Her body ached as though someone had beat her like a carpet and left her outside hanging on a line. Every muscle hurt, and her mind was fuzzy. It was all she could do to give him a weak smile and refrain from bursting into sobs and hugging the place in her chest where a gaping hole had opened up to swallow her from the inside out.

"I...." She shook her head and rubbed her eyes. "It was just a bad dream. I'm sorry if I scared you."

"Mom sent me up to get you," he said. "Breakfast is almost done."

"Tell her I'll be down soon."

Fritz nodded and turned to go. At her door, he paused. "Don't worry about your dream. It'll go away. Mine always do." His eyes brightened. "Especially with food. Mom made eggs and biscuits, and Dad brought home a whole bag of oranges from the Andersons' tree! And Godfather even brought bacon!" He let out a whoop and sprinted downstairs.

At the mention of her godfather, Clara's mind cleared. She

got out of bed, washed her face, brushed her hair, and dressed as fast as she could, mismatching her buttons three times before her dress was on straight. If anyone could straighten this nightmare out, it would be him.

The smells of coffee, eggs, bacon, and bread greeted her as she hurried downstairs, nearly tripping twice along the way. But when she reached the foot of the stairs, she realized there was something else she needed to do first.

"Oh, there you are." Clara's father found her kneeling in front of the Christmas tree, ferociously moving packages out from underneath it. "What are you doing?"

"I can't find my nutcracker."

"Your what?"

Clara sighed as she pulled out the last box. "The nutcracker that Fritz broke. I can't find it."

"Well, I'm sure it's somewhere in the house. You didn't go anywhere last night."

Oh, if only she had.

"Come on," he said, gently pulling her to her feet. "You'll feel better after you've had something to eat."

Breakfast really was a wonderful spread, far more decadent than what they'd grown used to over the course of the war. Not only were there all the foods Fritz had described, but her mother had also added one of her precious jars of cherry preserves, cinnamon rolls, and a big, freshly squeezed pitcher of orange juice. Fritz looked as though he might eat himself to death, judging by the fierce joy in his dark eyes, and Drosselmeyer and her mother were chatting away as she and her father took their seats.

Clara probably would have enjoyed the meal greatly if she hadn't spent the whole time fighting the feeling that wherever she had been, James still was. And that wherever that was, he was still alone. Ultimately, the guilt of knowing she'd hesitated when facing the choice that should have been the easiest of her life devastated her.

"Clara." Her mother interrupted her somber thoughts. Her gray eyes flicked down to Clara's empty plate. "Aren't you going to eat something? I know how much you like my cherry preserves. That's why I brought up a jar."

"Oh, of course," Clara gave her mother another weak smile. "I'm sorry. I just didn't sleep well—"

The telephone rang.

"That's probably your grandmother," her mother said as she stood to answer it.

As soon as her mother was gone, Clara's godfather cleared his throat. "So." He fixed his eyes on hers and folded his hands under his chin. "You didn't sleep well last night?"

Clara shook her head and stuffed a spoonful of eggs into her mouth. They had looked soft and fluffy on her plate, but they were unusually dry as she chewed them.

His piercing gaze didn't waver. "Your mother said you were sleeping soundly when she checked on you."

Clara nearly laughed in spite of herself. Leave it to her mother to check on her at twenty-one years old.

"About what time did you go to sleep?"

She hesitated. Reliving the night over and over again in her head was one thing, but sharing such an intimate dream or wish or whatever it had been with her entire family was another. "The clock woke me up at midnight," she said slowly, glancing at her father, who seemed engrossed in his newspaper. She lowered her voice and leaned closer. "I realized I'd forgotten my nutcracker downstairs, so I went to look for it."

Drosselmeyer's eyes glittered. For the first time, though, Clara realized they had dark circles beneath them. "Well, you know what they say, that the spell often ends at midnight." He picked up a biscuit and began spreading the cherry preserves on it. "Perhaps yours wasn't ending. But rather, it was beginning."

Clara nearly forgot to swallow as she gaped at her godfather. That he was up to something, she had no doubt. But with her father and brother in the room, she didn't dare ask. She needed to get him alone as soon as she could.

"Clara," her mother called as she walked back into the dining room. "I just received a very strange call from the hospital."

"Cape Fear?" Clara took a sip of her juice.

"Yes, from your friend, Sue."

Clara froze, her glass of orange juice perched on her lips.

Her mother frowned and put her hands on the back of Clara's chair. "It appears there's a patient who arrived last night at Walter Reed. He was transported from a European hospital to Maryland. They didn't even know he was coming until he arrived last night."

Clara tried to speak, but her voice failed her. Thankfully, her father asked instead. "Is it James?"

Everyone, even Fritz, was silent. Clara's mother sighed.

"They don't know. He's in a coma."

It was a good thing Clara was already seated.

"He doesn't have any identifying information on him," her mother continued. "All they can tell is that he's an American. But...." She paused, her eyes fixed sharply on Clara's face. "He does match James's description."

Clara choked on her juice. Her father jumped out of his chair and slapped her on the back until she waved him away. Then she stood and began to clear her plate. "I'll go wrap up breakfast."

Her father folded his paper. "Alright, Fritz. Hurry up. You know the drill."

"So we're going?" Fritz mumbled around the half-eaten pastry sticking out from his mouth.

"Yep," their father said. "Finish your breakfast and get your coat and shoes."

"What about our presents?" Fritz whined.

"Presents can wait," their father said.

"I have an idea." Clara turned to her little brother. "How about we take along my present for you, and you can open it on the way?"

Fritz was quite pleased with that idea, so when everyone was finally done eating, he grabbed his present, and everyone got ready to pile into the car.

But as Clara grabbed her coat and scarf and the men went outside to warm the car, her mother took her hand and motioned for her to wait.

"Clara," she said, staring down at their hands, "before we go, there's... there's something I need to ask you."

"Okay." Clara glanced back in the direction of the door. "But Dad says we need to get going soon."

"I know...." She sucked in a deep breath and stared at the ceiling. "I know you want it to be him. And I do, too. But... but what if it's not him?"

"Then," Clara said slowly, "we'll come home and hope it's him the next time." She paused when she saw the look on her mother's face. "Why?"

"I don't know." Her mother ran her fingers through her hair. "I just... I can't help wondering if maybe this is a bad idea."

"You mean you don't want me to go?"

"It's not that." Her mother sighed. But then she stopped and stood straighter. "You know what? Actually, that is what I'm saying."

"But—"

"Baby, I know you want him home. And you know what? I do, too! I want it so much! We all love him, you know that! I just...." She put her hand over her eyes and shook her head. "I just don't know if I can bear watching your dreams die...again. I just can't do it."

Neither of them spoke for a long time. Clara did her best to focus on breathing in and out evenly while her mother cried.

"So." Clara struggled to swallow. "You're asking me to give up."

Her mother put her bags down and gently took Clara's face in her hands. "We have gone to so many hospitals up and down the coast. And every time it's not him, I have to watch my daughter die a little inside." She glared at Clara. "And don't tell me you don't. Because I know that look you get when you see another young soldier brought back, and it's not him. And I just can't bear to see that happen one more time!" She finally stopped, her face pinched as she looked miserably at Clara.

"But what if it is him?" Clara whimpered. "We can't just leave him!"

Her mother said nothing, just frowned at the ground.

"What if," Clara said, feeling as though she were grasping at vapors, "we agree that if it's not him, we'll take a break from hospital visits. At least, of this kind."

"I don't know if you can do that, Clara," her mother said, shaking her head. "I think at the end of the day, you'll have to choose all or nothing. Are you going to wait forever, or are you going to start living again?"

Her father honked the horn from outside, but Clara couldn't bring herself to wave from the window. Her chest hurt as though someone had kicked it.

"What if," her mother said slowly, "we go today the way we always do. If James is there, we'll bring him back ourselves. But if it's not him," she reached up and touched Clara's face softly, "you look for a way to move on."

"Why?"

"Because you can't keep living like this."

"So what?" Clara folded her arms across her chest, unable to keep the biting sarcasm from her voice. "So you can force me to marry Edward?" As much as she cared about Edward, she would never be able to marry him. Not after last night.

"Marry Edward or don't marry him!" Her mother threw her hands up in the air. "But at some point in your life, you'll need to take off the ring!" She began to get excited, much to Clara's annoyance. "You can move up with Grandma and Grandpa Frank in New York if you want! Find a new normal! You did well in your studies, and I have no doubt you could get any job you wanted." Her voice fell to nearly a whimper. "I just can't watch you wither away anymore."

Clara's voice caught in her throat. She had been ready to turn around and walk out the door until she heard the tears in her mother's voice. They reminded her of the tears James had shed, and she was forced to recall the last moments of her dream the night before. It had seemed so real, every minute. The colors, smells, and sounds had been so vivid and would be imprinted on her memory forever. James had been as large as life itself.

But... what if it wasn't real? What if, instead, it was her tired mind trying to tell her she couldn't hang on any longer? Ann had said she would have to choose. Maybe this was the choice her heart had been trying to warn her about. Just as James had been torn from her by Fritz's soft voice, maybe her heart was no longer able to keep on hoping.

Truly, how much longer could she search? She felt wearier now than ever before, even during the war. As much as she hated to admit it, her mother was right. She couldn't keep running like this forever. Since he'd gone, she had pushed herself to stay busy every minute of every day. Falling asleep too tired to dream was her greatest reward, but that only revived her for another day to do it all over again.

Was that the meaning of her dream? Just as James had been unable to beat the darkness, maybe she was no longer able to deny the truth of his death?

Suddenly, without her permission, she realized she was nodding. "Fine," she whispered, closing her eyes. "This is the last one."

Her father honked again, and Clara turned to leave, her feet and heart wooden. She could feel her mother's concerned gaze, but she couldn't bring herself to meet it. She felt as though she'd become the betrayer and the betrayed, and if she wasn't careful, she might say something she regretted. It was the most she could do to get in the car next to her godfather and shut the door behind her.

As they rode, she fumbled nervously with the buttons on her jacket. In her rush to leave, she had forgotten to button it. But after her trembling fingers failed to properly close the third button four times, she gave up and crossed her arms with a huff. As she did, however, she couldn't help noticing the unusual pallor on Drosselmeyer's face. She leaned in closer to get a better look.

"Godfather, are you feeling well?"

He gave her a grin, but it didn't touch his eyes. "I'm an old man, Clara. Nothing on me is well." Then he chuckled. "I'm lucky anything on me is working these days at all."

Clara's mother turned around from the front seat and studied him as well. "I think Clara's right. Perhaps while we're at the hospital, we should get you looked at."

But Drosselmeyer waved them both off. "Let's just get up there and see this boy." He winked at Clara. "See if he's fit to utter our dear Clara's sweet name, or if he's just another rotten mongrel like the rest of them."

The drive to Walter Reed was long, over seven hours. But no matter how hard she tried, Clara's mind refused to focus. It bounced back and forth between memories from the night before and what she knew to be true here in real life.

That James had been spiraling down fast was obvious. From their reuniting to their separation, he'd changed from a competent soldier, determined to defend and protect, to a man incapable of caring for even himself. And yet... there had been moments, like in the pub and on the field, when she had glimpsed him, her own true James. And those moments cut her heart more deeply than the others.

"What are you thinking about?"

"What?" Clara looked up to see her godfather studying her again with those knowing eyes. The sky was losing light fast, day giving way to twilight. But even in the weakening light, she knew he hadn't missed a thing.

"You're twisting your hair. You're upset about something." He glanced over at the other passengers. Clara's mother and Fritz were sleeping, and her father was busy fiddling with the radio dial as he drove. "Do you have something you want to tell me?"

Clara took her ring off and rubbed the three diamonds between her fingers. She wasn't sure she could let it go even if the man at the hospital wasn't James. The ring had become her one constant in life. When she needed something to hold on to, James's promise was there.

Unlike she had been for him.

"Last night," she said slowly, "I had a dream."

"Yes?"

She opened her mouth, but nothing came out. What was wrong with her? Why was she even entertaining the crazy idea that these might be real memories? Finding someone in a dream was impossible. Before she could answer, though, her father called out, "We're here!"

They pulled into a parking spot in front of the hospital, and

Clara realized she had no more breath with which to speak. *It's impossible,* she chided herself over and over again as they climbed out and walked toward the building. *You know it's impossible and getting your hopes up will only disappoint you further when he's not there.* Every word, every touch had seemed so real at the time, but the closer they got, the more she knew it had been just that... a dream. She would simply have to content herself in knowing she now had the chance to help a hapless young man in the way she hoped others might have helped James if they'd had the chance. Coma or none, she and her family could at least give him a Christmas that wasn't completely alone.

They stopped at an information desk, and Clara's father explained the situation to the nurse. The nurse's face lit up, and her black curls bobbed as she jumped up from her chair. "Oh yes!" Her eyes moved immediately to Clara. "The whole hospital's talking about it. It's like a love story from a novel!"

"If it's really him," her mother interjected gently.

Fritz made a sour face, and Clara's face burned as several other nurses within hearing distance seemed to lean closer. How much had Sue told her contact? Now not only was she about to face the greatest disappointment of her life, but the entire hospital might be watching. She couldn't do anything about it now, though. Soon everyone would know it wasn't James, and the gossip would die.

Their shoes made eerie tapping sounds on the floor as the nurse led them down several halls. When they finally arrived at the room, Clara kept her eyes away from the bed as her family filed inside. Not that she needed to. A curtain hung between the bed and the door, hiding the patient on the other side.

"He hasn't actually awakened," the nurse said as she moved around the bed and leaned over it. "But now, maybe...." She reappeared and rolled back the curtain.

YES, SIR

Chaos ensued. Clara's mother threw her hands over her mouth. Drosselmeyer began coughing, and Fritz hollered as their father desperately tried to calm him down, all the while muttering to himself about impossibilities and odds. Nurses had gathered at the door and were starting to spill into the room, whispering amongst themselves as they tried to get a good look at the patient and his visitor.

But Clara hardly heard any of it.

Because there on the bed was James.

Her hands shook as she reached for him. The weak light of the lamp on his bedside table accentuated the lines on his face even more than in her dream, particularly the scars. His body, which had been full and muscled when he'd left, looked thin and weak beneath the hospital sheets.

But it was him.

On the heels of her ecstasy, fear and bitter disappointment followed. For though his chest still rose and fell beneath the sheets, his breaths were shallow, and his eyes remained shut. She had found him again only to learn that he was still lost.

"What's wrong with him?" Clara's mother pressed one hand

over her heart, the other worrying a lock of her hair like she was going to pull it out.

"He's still in a coma, I'm afraid." The nurse pursed her lips. "Head injury. And even since he was delivered here last night, his breathing is getting more shallow."

"Of course," Clara whispered to herself, closing her eyes. A coma. The darkness. The confusion. Just as she'd suspected, he was trapped. She just hadn't considered his entrapment to be anything like this.

It was just a dream after all. And it was only a coincidence that her dream had been right.

"So," the nurse said, bending to make eye contact with Clara. "Is this him?"

Unable to form a coherent response, Clara nodded.

The nurses outside the room began to squeal and chatter, but their nurse ignored the hullabaloo.

"Talk to him, honey." She gave Clara a little shove closer to the bed. "See if he can hear you."

"Do you have a telephone I can use?" Her mother asked, face still white. "I need to call his parents."

"They're with his sister in Connecticut," Clara called back absently.

"If you go with Cindy here," the nurse pointed to a tall woman in the hall, "you can help her with the identification details. And you two." She took Fritz by the shoulder and Clara's father by the elbow and gave Clara a wink. "I think there are some Christmas cookies in the break room we need help eating. The rest of you, out." She shooed away the remaining nurses still lingering in the doorway.

Soon the room was finally empty of everyone but Clara and Drosselmeyer, who had fallen asleep in one of the chairs in the corner. Clara swallowed and moved cautiously toward the bed.

"James," she whispered. "James... it's me. Clara."

He didn't so much as twitch, his handsome face as still as a stone angel carved into a tomb. She tried again.

"James, I don't know if you remember last night. Maybe you don't. Maybe it was all in my head, but…." She drew in a shuddering breath. "I remember. And it made me miss you more than ever." She paused. "There's so much I need to tell you." She could feel the tears running down her face, but she was smiling. For him, she would smile. "On the way, I thought up names for our three girls. And one for the boy. And I think we'll get a dog, too. Not too big, not too small. I know you like big dogs, but I don't want to be stepping in clumps of fur all the time, and I won't have him chewing the furniture legs." Tears streamed down her face, but now she was laughing as she sat on the edge of the bed and clutched at his arm.

"Now that the war's over, they're planning a new housing development over on the north side of town, and I saw some of the plans the other day at the library. They're not going to be big houses, but they look clean and neat, and I think they'll be lovely. Perfect for a little family like ours. And you can build us a picket fence, and I can get a new job. Actually, Mr. Peters was talking about hiring me on full-time. He…."

But her voice broke. She couldn't go on. She couldn't keep pretending everything was alright. She had finally gotten him back, and now he was gone again, nearly as gone as he had been before. Clara knew very little about head injuries, but she did know that many never healed. So many soldiers had died not because of a bullet or a knife, but rather because they'd been hit on the head or had fallen the wrong way.

"Clara."

She looked over her shoulder to see Drosselmeyer's eyes open as he gestured weakly for her to come near. His head remained back against the wall, and his voice was thin. She got up and knelt beside his chair, taking his hand in hers.

"Your hands are cold!" She reached up to feel his forehead, but he shook his head and gave her a tired smile.

"I never told you this, but I've been a godfather to many children."

Clara frowned. "How? You're not that old."

"Ah, but that's where you're wrong, my dear." He patted her head. "You see, a long time ago, so long you'd never believe me if I told you, I was given a gift. And that gift was my very own Christmas magic."

"But Father and Mother said you're—"

"That's the beauty about magical gifts. Adults often can't see them because they don't believe magic exists. They simply accept whatever they've been told and move on." His eyes twinkled, despite the dark shadows beneath them. "Your parents never knew how old I truly am because they never asked. To them, I'm the sweet old man who lives next door and dotes on their children. But you...." He smiled and squeezed her hands. "You were always my favorite. You always knew I was something more."

"But I'm all grown up now, too."

"And that's what I've always loved about you." He chuckled. "You might think you're quite grown up and practical, but underneath that perfectly polished young woman is a child that refused to disappear completely with childhood."

Clara could think of nothing to say to that.

"I've wondered for a long time how I was going to use the remnants of my Christmas magic. You see, before you were born, I had used most of it up on the other children I watched over. But I kept a little bit stored up because I knew that my last magic had to be my best. It had to be for a cause more noble than little wooden nutcrackers or making the very toy a child wanted most appear under his tree."

"Godfather, what are you talking about?"

With great effort, he leaned forward and kissed her on the top of her head. "I'm saying that I've found the perfect Christmas miracle to be my last." Then he leaned back and rested his head against the wall and gave her a tired smile.

But Clara most certainly was not ready for a goodbye of any kind. She gripped his hands and squeezed, as if keeping them warm would change his mind.

"Come now," he said, peeling her hands away. "Don't make my last moments here a time of tears."

"You're not leaving me." She pouted and shook her head like a child. "I can't lose you, too!"

"You're not losing me," he whispered. "You'll see me again when it's time for you to leave this earth as well. But until then, I want you to promise me a Christmas gift of my own."

"I'm not promising you anything because you're not leaving!"

"Even if it means spending the rest of your life with James?"

Clara couldn't have moved if she'd tried.

Her godfather took advantage of her shock, leaned forward, and whispered in her ear. "Promise me you'll never take a minute with him for granted." Then he chuckled. "And maybe tell your little ones of your old Godfather Drosselmeyer one day. So they'll know who I am when they get to Heaven, too." He leaned his head against the wall again and closed his eyes.

"Wait!" Clara cried.

He opened an eye. "What?"

"Last night…." She took a deep breath. "That was you, wasn't it? My dream about James." It sounded ludicrous speaking it out loud, but her godfather's grin only widened.

"That depends on whether or not you believe me."

She frowned. That wasn't the answer she wanted.

"But Clara?"

"Yes?"

He paused. "Whether or not you believe me doesn't change the fact that he doesn't have much time left. Give him a reason to stay. And make sure he's reminded of that every single day."

With those words, her godfather winked and closed his eyes for the last time. Then his chest rose and fell one more time. And it didn't move again.

Clara ran to yell for a nurse. But as she reached the doorpost, she heard another voice behind her.

"Clara?"

For one long second, Clara was caught between worlds. In one, she watched her childhood pass away, the part she hadn't known still existed. And in the other, she was staring across the room into the eyes of her future. And the future's eyes were a startling blue.

Suddenly, despite her doubts and all the scientific probabilities of what should be and could be didn't mean a thing. Because her godfather had gotten Clara her Christmas miracle. Before she knew what she was doing, Clara crossed the room in one leap and was in the arms of her soldier.

And that soldier was kissing her with more passion than ever before.

After an eternal moment of feeling his lips move against hers, his hands in her hair and all over her face, she pulled back to look at him. Dark shadows hung below his red, watery eyes, making him look as though he hadn't slept in years, as if gazing at her was taking all the energy he had. But she didn't care. Because her soldier was alive.

He traced her face with his fingertips before pulling her down to kiss her again. But Clara had to know something first.

"Last night…." she whispered, her breath ragged with nerves. "Do you remember—"

"I remember everything."

Clara laughed, tears spilling from her face and mingling with his.

A nurse walked in. "What's all this...?" Her eyes widened when she saw them, then she whirled around. "Get the doctor!" she yelled into the hall.

"But how?" Clara asked the nurse, her face still wet with tears as the nurse began examining him. "How did they find him?"

"An odd story you are." The nurse nodded at James as she leaned in to poke and prod in a few places before scribbling notes on her clipboard. "Out of the blue last night, an ambulance arrived with a comatose patient. Apparently, they knew you were a GI, but you must have lost your dog tags somewhere. When you were taken to one of the European hospitals, your uniform was torn so badly no one could identify you or your division. They knew you were an American, but that's all. And since you were in a coma, you weren't going to be answering questions anytime soon." She glanced through her papers before nodding once to herself.

"But how did he get here?" Clara asked, taking his hand and holding it tightly.

"They decided to transfer him here for some reason, though why they did it right before Christmas instead of months ago is beyond me."

"Was...." Clara felt foolish for asking it, but she had to. "Was he here all night last night?"

The nurse let out a short laugh. "Of course! Where else do you think a comatose patient would be?"

Clara didn't answer. Instead, she and James shared a long look before she glanced back at Drosselmeyer again. A serene smile still graced his face.

The nurse followed her gaze and dropped her clipboard. "What's happened to him?"

Clara gazed back at James. "He went home," she said softly.

The nurse, of course, was not as sure as Clara. She called in more nurses and doctors to take her godfather away and assess him, but Clara knew he was gone. Just the way he had wanted to be. How he had done it, she would never know, nor would she fully understand his Christmas magic. But she would be forever grateful. And for some strange reason, though she would miss him as long as she lived, she was at peace.

When the fuss over Drosselmeyer had moved to another room, and Clara's parents had been called, the doctor finally arrived to check on James. His examination was even more thorough than the nurse's, and Clara had to stand behind the curtain for propriety's sake. When the doctor was done, though, and the curtain was rolled back, he informed them that James's recovery was nothing short of miraculous. The doctor had no real explanation.

"All I can say," he said as he took off his glasses and cleaned them on his coat, "is that you, son, have been given a second chance. If I were you, I would use it wisely. I'll be honest, though. It's going to take a long time for you to heal. And you'll need help."

James thanked the doctor but said nothing else until the door was shut. As soon as they were alone, his smile disappeared, and he traced her wrist with his fingers.

"He's right, you know," he said softly. "I'm not the same man you said yes to." His voice dropped even lower. "But you knew that last night. I don't even know when the dream started or ended. I just... I know I said things I shouldn't have...."

Clara knew he was thinking of their argument about Edward. A long moment passed before either of them spoke.

"June," she finally said.

"What?" He looked at her, but she kept her eyes on their hands.

"You wrote your last letter on the first of June last year. You were preparing to go to Normandy, or so we figured out afterward. You couldn't tell us much in the letter, but I knew something big was coming. And then neither I nor your parents heard anything after that. Whenever we asked, we were told that some people simply couldn't be found." She leaned forward to kiss him on the cheek. Her heart broke a little, though, when he turned away and groaned.

"This is all wrong." He scrunched his eyes shut and rubbed them. "I never wanted this for you!"

She tried not to let the disappointment show on her face as she sat back. "I don't understand."

"Before I left, I prayed for nothing more than that you would wait for me while I was gone."

Clara's conscience pricked her. "I promise, I really did try." She felt dirty for even considering Edward yesterday.

James ran his fingers along her brow bone. Her skin burned beneath his touch. "You did," he said, "And you did it so well that when I didn't come back, you never moved on." He ran his hand through his hair. "It's not fair to you."

"Now, hold on—"

"I mean, I've been stuck in this...." He shook his head and looked up at the ceiling. "It's like I'm stuck in—"

"In what?" she said softly. "Darkness?"

He stared at her before nodding slowly. "Every once in a while, I'd surface from the dream. No one could hear me, and I could barely hear them. I mean, I might make out a voice here or there, but usually, it was all just a haze. Sights and sounds blended together." He met her eyes and shrugged helplessly. "And even if I did know where I was, I've done things, Clara. I've seen...." He took a deep shuddering breath and leaned his head back and closed his eyes. "The war changed me, and I'm broken now."

His voice cracked, and with it, her heart.

"I thought that if I got home, everything could go back to the way it used to be." He shook his head, and his voice came out in a whisper. "But now that I know the truth, you deserve so much better than what I've become." He paused, eyes still closed. "I wouldn't blame you now if you decided to walk away from me. I wish I could."

So this was the choice Ann had warned her about. Everything that had happened the night before had been preparing her for this moment.

Last night had emptied her of all self-righteous assurance that she could save him. Seeing him weeping on the bridge had proven she wasn't enough to heal him. No matter how much she wanted to, she couldn't undo the war. The rats would always be there inside. Ann had been right about that.

But Ann had also asked her if she would be able to live with him. And while Clara knew now that she couldn't fix him, only another miracle of God could do that, she could live with him. She could live, and she could make sure he lived, too. She wasn't strong enough to pull him out, but she could walk alongside him. He could lean on her the way she'd leaned on him. It wouldn't be perfect. But nothing ever was.

Her heart had shattered with his confession, and the pieces had fallen one at a time into her stomach.

And yet... no. She wasn't going to let it end like this. She wouldn't. Not after the torture she'd just lived through for the last day, fearing she'd left him to die alone and afraid. She was never going to feel that way again. Instead, she grabbed his face with both hands and leaned down until their foreheads touched.

"Now, you listen to me, James Matthew Parker!" Resistance darkened his eyes, but she ignored it. "I'll have none of this self-pity."

"Clara— "

"You may very well be broken, but I think it's up to me whether or not that matters. Now you were right. I lied."

His eyes widened, but he didn't interrupt. He at least had enough sense to know better than that.

"You said I hit you with that baseball on purpose. And do you know what? I did. Because I might have been young, but I knew the makings of a good man when I saw one. And I panicked when I realized you were looking at Cathy. I wanted you to look at me. And since then, I have never looked back." She held up her left hand and jabbed a finger at the ring. "And when you asked me to marry you and I said yes, I fully intended to take you for every day of your life until death did us part. For better or for worse, and if this... brokenness you carry doesn't count as worse, I don't know what does."

"But—"

"I don't care how long it takes, we're going to work together to put you back in one piece. And I— "

Before she could finish, he enveloped her in a tight embrace, and his lips covered hers like the burning rays of golden sun against the surface of sparkling untouched snow. He buried a hand in her hair as they kissed, while his other hand pressed against her back, holding her close. As his mouth moved tenderly against hers, she felt him whisper, "I love you, Clara."

She clung to him even more tightly, wrapping her arms around his shoulders, relishing in the way it felt to trace the familiar lines in the nape of his neck.

"Well, this is certainly a way to feel more like yourself."

They turned to see the doctor standing in the doorway, looking amused. Clara's face burned, but James just broke into his cockiest grin.

"Yes, sir. I think it is."

EPILOGUE: MISSION

ONE YEAR LATER...

"*Y*ou ready for this?" Clara asked as she pressed the doorbell. She carefully scanned his face as he clutched the presents like life preservers. His jaw was tight and his eyes a little too bright, but he nodded.

"Yes."

She inwardly sighed. A year had passed since he came home, and though he was making tremendous progress, even beginning his teaching degree, large gatherings with lots of noise and movement were still hard on him. She had the feeling they would be for a long time.

"Hey." She wove her arm through his and smiled up at him. "You're with family. They'll understand if you need to step out. And who knows, you might have fun. You used to love my family's Christmas Eve party."

He only gave her a sharp nod and turned back to the door as it opened.

"They're here!" her father called over his shoulder before coming out and simultaneously embracing Clara while shaking hands with James.

Her family descended upon them as soon as they stepped in, just as she had known they would. And to his credit, James played the part. The stress disappeared from his face. He grinned at everyone, kissed all the mothers, aunts, and grand-mothers on the cheeks, and playfully punched the little boys on the arms. The men pulled him into their conversation about President Truman's most recent policies. Was he actually having fun the way he appeared to be? She couldn't tell. But she hoped so.

"Clara!" Her mother ran over and dragged her to the corner where all the women were gathered. "Did you see Aunt Pearl's engagement ring?"

"Engagement ring?" Clara grabbed her aunt's outstretched hand and gasped. "Auntie, it's beautiful!" Then what her mother had said dawned on her. "Wait, you're getting married?"

Everyone laughed, and Aunt Pearl grabbed her up into a hug.

"He's a retired colonel!" Clara's Grandmother Hannah said with a proud smile. "He said he laid eyes on her and was never leaving North Carolina again."

"It's just because all the other women my age were nabbed up by the time he got back." Aunt Pearl rolled her eyes. "That, and he likes my cookies." Still, she looked rather smug.

Aunt Marla sniffed. "With the war good and over, I'm assuming the wedding will be far nicer than Clara's."

"Oh no." Aunt Pearl winked at Clara. "The entire town won't be showing up to see my groom."

Clara returned the smile. It was probably true. There hadn't been a wedding like Clara's since the town could remember. Everything about the wedding had been magical and even a little mysterious, including the events leading up to their nuptials.

Drosselmeyer had indeed been pronounced dead in the hospital. The nurses had fluttered about muttering to one another how dreadful they felt that someone should have passed away under their care and been mistaken for sleeping. But Clara had known. She'd been holding his hand as the life had left him. And though she missed him terribly, she knew he had been ready to go.

They'd buried Drosselmeyer the next week, the soonest her family could set his funeral. And while Clara wasn't surprised, after what he'd shared with her in the hospital, her parents found it quite odd that no living relatives could be located.

"It's as if we're the closest thing to a family he had!" Clara's mother exclaimed after hanging up the phone from her sixth inquiry. "The house was paid for in full ages ago. He had no bank accounts or even a bill with the grocer!"

Clara just listened dutifully. Her mother wouldn't believe her even if Clara told her the truth. For it was Clara's secret, and outside of Fritz and James, there was no one else with whom she really needed to share. No one else would believe her anyway. But that was okay.

Upon the reading of his will, it had also been discovered that Clara and James didn't need to buy one of the new houses in the development north of town after all. For Drosselmeyer had left his house to them, and with it, a surprisingly large lump of cash, exactly enough with which to pay for their wedding and buy a car as soon as the factories started producing them again.

The wedding had been enchanting. Clara's dress was like that of a fairy, its glass beading throwing sparkles around the sanctuary like the coating of a sugarplum. Their first Sunday school teacher had cried and claimed she'd known they were destined for each other since that first class when they were six. The pastor, during the ceremony, said he'd known they were meant to be together from the time they took confirmation class when they were thirteen. Even Aunt Marla had been forced to admit that the wedding was unusually moving, though she did add that the bride seemed just a bit too enchanted with the groom, and the groom made eyes at the bride's figure a little too often for taste.

"It's going to be wonderful!" Clara gave her aunt another hug. "I couldn't be happier for you."

The other women joined in with their agreements, but as talk turned to the guest list and dress and what kind of food would be served, Clara's eyes strayed to James.

He was good at pretending, probably because he did it a lot. Her family even commented on it often, how they could barely tell he'd ever been injured at all. As soon as he'd been released from the hospital, he'd announced that he was going to be a teacher, much to the chagrin of his parents, and he had started school right away. He was so ambitious and dedicated to his studies, her parents liked to boast to their friends, and he was just as much a smart aleck as he had ever been.

But Clara knew. She knew that at night he lay awake for hours, afraid to sleep for the nightmares. Sudden noises startled him still, and he often sat staring blankly at the wall, uninterested in the things he and Clara used to enjoy the most. And as he cycled through his moods and reactions, she often worked through her own as well. Anger at God for allowing her husband to hurt so much. Sorrow for his daily suffering as she begged for him to be healed. Loneliness when he tuned her out and didn't hear a word she said. Joy and thanksgiving on the good days when he was himself before it all started again.

Even now, his jaw tensed as the men pressed him to solve one of their disagreements about the war. He kept the smile on his face, but it was growing more and more forced.

She took a deep breath as she grabbed a package from

beneath the tree and two blankets from a nearby cupboard. Tonight was going to be the start of something new. Because she wasn't going to let anything steal the beauty of this evening from her. Not shell shock or Aunt Marla or the ache for her beloved godfather.

"Alright, everyone," she laughed as she took James's hand. "I'm going to steal my husband for a few minutes."

The family, busy with talk of Aunt Pearl and her fiancé, who had made an appearance as well, let them go without too much protesting. She led James out the back door, and holding hands, they walked to the beach. She stopped where the tide couldn't reach them and handed him the blankets she'd grabbed on the way out. He spread one on the sand then helped her sit down on it before spreading the second over them both. As soon as he was seated, she nestled under his arm to hide from the cold evening air.

He stared out at the waves, absently stroking her arm with his fingers.

"Where are you?" she said softly.

He hesitated before answering. "Ann's house," he finally said. "Guess I was hoping their father made it back."

Clara nodded and left it at that. The waves crashed rhythmically below them, and she closed her eyes and basked in the sound. She'd wondered about Ann's family as well, especially after James had assured her that they were real people, and he really did spend a Christmas with them. Though Ann, he promised her, was actually just a precocious little girl, not an angel or fairy or anything else unusual.

"I'm also pretty sure your Aunt Marla is trying to kill me," he continued.

Clara opened her eyes and laughed. "Why is that?"

"She made me eat that purple glop—"

"Oh, James," Clara groaned. "You're not supposed to eat Aunt

Marla's plum pudding." She turned to look up at him with mock solemnity. "Ever. No one eats Marla's pudding."

He made a face. "I'm pretty sure I tasted frogs."

She laughed again, then sat up to study him more closely. "I mean it, though. How are you doing?"

He sucked in a deep breath and blew it out slowly, and she wondered what he saw as he stared at the fading horizon. "Some days are good. Like today." He nodded once. "But other days are hard. It's like…." Then he shrugged and huffed. "I don't know how to put it into words."

"That's okay," she said softly. "Take your time."

He didn't talk after that. She began to despair of ever getting an answer when he finally whispered, "A lot of things about the army were bad. The rations, the training, the fighting. But at least whenever we felt lost, there was a mission. We always knew what we were supposed to be doing, whether it was cleaning the latrines or doing push-ups or jumping out of planes. We always had a mission, and when life crashed and that mission failed, we had another to take its place." He played with a lock of her hair as she leaned against him, not taking his eyes off the water. "Now I feel like life is still crashing, but I've got no mission. I'm just… floating away. Like I'm in the Zeppelin. And sometimes I'm afraid I'll never be able to get back down to everyone else."

Clara's heart twisted as she listened. A year had passed, and only now was she even beginning to understand his pain. How much more was there that he wasn't telling her? But then she took a deep breath and closed her eyes briefly to clear her head. Tonight wasn't about getting lost with her husband and his thoughts. It was about throwing him a rope. One she prayed was long enough to reach him.

She turned and picked up the little gift she'd brought with

her and handed it to him. He took the box wrapped in string and newspaper and gave her a look of surprise.

"I was going to save it until later when everyone else exchanges gifts, but I think you should open it now."

He turned it over in his hands for a moment before pulling off the string. She bit her lip and tapped her fingers on her legs as he lifted the lid.

"What's this?" He pulled the baseball out of the box and frowned at it. She could almost hear his thoughts. They had at least a bucketful of balls behind their house already.

"This is your next mission."

He gave her an odd look, so she smiled and took the ball.

"Your mission, sergeant, is to live each day as fully as you can until you teach our baby how to throw this ball."

He stared at the ball for a long minute before comprehension dawned on his face. Warmth filled Clara's chest as, for a brief moment, the haunted look left his face, and all that was left was boyish surprise. "You mean you're—"

She beamed. "Yep."

He looked back and forth between her belly and her face so fast that she laughed again. "How long?" he whispered, his hand hovering as though he wanted to touch but he was too afraid.

"Summer. July. Maybe August."

His mouth opened and closed, but no sounds came out.

"And when you accomplish that mission," she said, placing the ball back in his hand, "your next mission will be to throw the ball with our baby until he has a baby of his own." She smiled. "Then he'll need someone to show him how it's done all over again."

When she finished, though, he still looked so shocked she wondered how much of her little speech he had even heard. She sat up on her knees and turned to face him.

"I knew when I married you that this wasn't going to be easy.

But we're going to take each day at a time. You said you need a mission, well here it is." She took his hand and placed it on her belly. "And don't you think for a minute," she let her voice grow sharp, "that if you get distracted and start shirking your responsibility, I won't throw this at you—"

His mouth was on hers, warm and strong before she finished, and he wound his arms around her, lifting her off the blanket and onto his lap. There was heat in his touch that hadn't been there in a long time. His fingers explored her face, her neck, her back, and shoulders. For a moment, she forgot it was Christmas. She was only aware that the man she loved was holding her close. And even if that man was still in hiding more often than not, he was here now. And she was thankful for that.

He broke off the kiss far sooner than she wanted and leaned his forehead against hers. "I'm going to do my best," he said breathlessly, his voice low and rough. "But I can't promise to do it all as well as I'd like." His eyes were shiny, and his words shook just a bit. "I'm not the man I was before."

Clara kissed his chin, then his cheek. "I don't want that man. I want you." He started to shake his head and mutter about weakness, but she pressed a finger to his lips. "We knew this was going to be tough. We agreed on that. But God gave us a second chance, and we're both going to do our best to make the most of it." Reaching up, she traced the shape of his face. "Your responsibility is to keep going. And mine is to be right there at your side. And until God brings us home, I'm afraid you're stuck with me."

He chuckled as he bent down to kiss her again. Then he stopped.

"But if I'm going to be teaching him baseball, what are you going to teach him?" The ornery quirk of his brow challenged her. "Don't think you're going to get off easy."

Clara pressed her lips softly against his and smiled into his kiss. "I'll tell him the story of how a lonely little girl found her missing nutcracker, and he came to life."

"Then what happened to them after that?"

"They lived happily ever after."

As soon as she'd said the words, he was kissing her again, and Clara uttered up a prayer of thanks to Heaven. Everything truly was going to be alright. No, better than alright.

It was her wish come true.

~

Dear Reader,

Thank you for journeying with me through Clara's Soldier. *To get a free short story about Clara and James, subscribe to my free newsletter at BrittanyFichterFiction.com. You'll get exclusive content and sneak peeks at my new books before they're published.*

Also, if you like enjoyed this book, it would be a huge help to me if you gave it an honest review on Amazon or Goodreads.com. Reviews help readers find my books, helping me write more books in turn.

For a sneak peek at my retelling of The Green-Eyed Prince, keep reading. But first things first . . . .

"SHELL SHOCK" OR POST-TRAUMATIC STRESS DISORDER

In WWII, what we now know as post-traumatic stress disorder (PTSD) was known as "shell shock." Doctors and the government knew it was linked to combat somehow, but that was really all they knew.

Today, we know more about PTSD than we did in the 1940's. Unfortunately, however, we're seeing greater numbers of American veterans and servicemen (and women) who are suffering as well.

According to Military.com's article, "VA Reveals its Veteran Suicide Statistic Included Active-Duty Troops," the American Veteran Affairs released a report stating 20 veterans, active duty members, reservists, and guardsmen commit suicide every day.

If you or a loved one need help, know you're not alone. In fact, here are several organizations you can contact for assistance. Asking for help dealing with the pain and scars might feel frustrating or even shameful. But getting help is far from cowardly. In fact, it's an act of courage that means you're doing whatever it takes to find healing and hope for both you and those you love.

In a crisis, contact:

- **911**
- Suicide Prevention Lifeline: **1-800-273-8255**
- Veterans Crisis Line: **1-800-273-8255**

To get more help from the U.S. Department of Veterans Affairs, visit them at https://www.ptsd.va.gov/public/where-to-get-help.asp .

For help finding a local faith-based counselor, contact:

The Association of Certified Biblical Counselors at 502-410-5526 or go to https://biblicalcounseling.com/about/contact/ .

THE GREEN-EYED PRINCE

A RETELLING OF THE FROG PRINCE

"There." Kartek gave the little girl's arm a quick squeeze and smiled. "You're ready to play Clump Ball again. Just be careful of the big boys this time. Sometimes they forget to look for brave little girls like you."

The girl gave Kartek a big toothy grin as her mother bowed. "I thank you, my jahira!" She patted her big belly. "I do not know what I would do without her." She smiled down at her daughter. "Sashi is my greatest help around the house now as we get ready for the baby."

Kartek nodded once. "May the Maker gift you a healthy, strong child and a safe delivery." She looked over at the line as the woman took her daughter and left. Before she called for the next in line, however, something to her left caught her eye. Careful not to appear alarmed, she waved over her bodyguard and nodded in the direction of the column of thick yellow smoke that was rising in the air.

"Ebo, what do you think that is?" she asked in a low voice.

Her bodyguard frowned. "No one knows. Fadil believes it is simply a brush fire, no closer than the river at most."

She frowned. True, a thunderstorm had moved through the valley the night before. Still, something bothered her, an uneasiness she couldn't quite put a name to. "The smoke is an odd color to be caused by a brush fire."

"Do you wish to cut this morning's healings short?" Oni, Kartek's favorite handmaiden, asked.

Kartek studied the smoke for another moment longer. Because of the high city walls, seeing its base location was impossible. Still, if there had been any real threat, Commander Fadil and Ebo would have swept her out of the public plaza long before. They had done it before during far less threatening situations. So she shook her head. "No, thank you. The line is short today. I will finish here as usual." She looked up at the line of people standing before her and put on her most reassuring smile. "Who is next?"

Truly, the line wasn't as long as it normally was. Sometimes, it wrapped so far around the pool and into the village that she had to move everyone back into the palace. She preferred to avoid healing inside, as having great numbers of citizens crowding about the throne room created more work for the palace staff. But the sun made it too hot to heal outside much after dawn, at least in the dry season. As there were only a dozen citizens still waiting their turn with her, however, she should be able to get through them all before the sun rose too high. So she dipped her hand in the water of the pool where she sat and rubbed it on her face.

A man approached her and bowed from the waist. "I thank you, Jahira, for seeing me."

"And what do you need healing for this morning?" she asked. He held out his hand, and Kartek leaned in closer to see the deep gash that ran across his palm. "How did you get this?"

"I was working in my garden when I tripped and fell on one of my tools."

Kartek nodded and reached for his hand. "Oni, a clean rag, please."

Her handmaiden handed her a rag, and Kartek dipped it into the jar of water beside her that Oni had brought for this very purpose. She held it over his palm and squeezed the water out so that it ran over the cut. Red water splashed onto the ground and the man clenched his jaw.

"I'm sorry for the pain," Kartek said as she laid the rag down and folded his hand gently into a fist. "But if I don't clean it, the healing won't be as thorough." Then, closing her eyes, she exhaled, letting the warmth run from her heart through her shoulders, down her arms, and into her fingers that held his. She heard him gasp, and she couldn't help smiling a bit. Though her eyes were closed, she could envision the familiar pink mist covering their hands.

It never ceased to amaze her, either.

"My jahira," Oni leaned in as the man thanked her profusely and the woman behind him came to the front of the line. "Seamstress needs to see you when you are finished."

Kartek's heart paused briefly before returning to its usual rhythm. "The wedding dress?"

Oni nodded, her brown eyes a little too bright with excitement.

Kartek sighed. "Very well. As soon as we are finished here." Suddenly, she was wishing the line of those waiting to be healed was far longer. No, that wouldn't do. She should be grateful that the Maker had kept her city safe from a great calamity or sickness through the night. Still, her gown fitting appointments hadn't held much allure for her since her parents had been—

No, she wasn't going to think about that, either.

The sun was peeking out from the barren craggy mountains in the distance as Kartek waved goodbye to her final subject and turned to go with Oni. Ebo hovered behind, too, of course, but that was nothing new. Kartek couldn't remember a time when Ebo hadn't hovered.

"You're nervous, aren't you?"

Kartek wanted to grimace at her friend's forward questions as they crossed the square toward the palace. But as she glanced up at Oni, however, a movement caught her eye. Kartek stopped walking and squinted.

"Did you see that?" Kartek asked, taking a few steps toward where the movement had been.

"No. Where?"

"There. At that back gate in the wall. The one the servants use to get to the fields."

Oni huffed and looked for a moment before shaking her head. "I see nothing. And do not try to change the subject. Every time we go to finalize more wedding details, you become less and less enthusiastic." She leaned in. "Are you nervous?"

Kartek stared at the now empty space where she had been sure she'd seen a face a moment before. The skin on her neck prickled. She considered going to Ebo, only to realize that her bodyguard was already on his way back from investigating. When he said nothing, though, she shook her head to herself and tried to pay attention to Oni once again.

"Well, are you?" Oni pressed.

Kartek pursed her lips as she considered how to answer. The jahira was never supposed to be nervous, or at least she was never supposed to show that she was anything less than perfectly at ease, a subject Ahmos had spent hours lecturing her about. But Oni knew her too well to be fooled, and they both knew it.

"I suppose it's beginning to seem more real," Kartek said, pitching her voice low.

"I should hope so!" Oni laughed. "You are to be married in a month! If you're not ready for it now, I don't know if you will ever be!" She grinned shamelessly. "I would be nervous. Your betrothed is so large and fearsome. Kissing him would be more like kissing a mountain than a man!"

"Oni!" Kartek hissed, trying to smother a giggle. "That is not an appropriate way to speak of the Rayis!" She glanced around as the palace doors swung open for them. "Or my future husband."

"It doesn't change anything." Oni smirked.

As if Kartek needed reminding. She hadn't seen her betrothed often, not more than twice a year since they'd been betrothed, but every time she saw Gahiji, he seemed to have grown in both muscles and height. Kartek tried to think of something else, but it was too late. She could already feel the red blush rise to her cheeks, which only made Oni laugh more.

The palace was already decidedly cooler than her spot at the pool had been, the six white open archways greeting her as she stepped inside. Servants scurried around. Music came from somewhere at the south end of the palace, and laughter was heard frequently as they moved up a set of spiraling sandstone steps, down one stone-laden hall, then another. As they walked and Oni continued to try and pull details out of Kartek, Kartek closed her eyes and drank in the tranquility of her home.

Compared to the castles of the north, particularly Destin's renowned Fortress, her sprawling palace was rather unprotected. Its wide entrance with its six arches and eight pillars opened up directly to the main city plaza, where their prized oasis pool sat, the heart of the city. Sandstone houses and shops surrounded the large plaza, which was nearly always filled with families shopping, vendors with carts, and curious travelers come to see the Jewel of the Desert, as the natural pool was often called. There were no moats, trenches, or even a gate to separate Kartek from her people. But really, with the wall that ran around the city, which stood three stories high and backed the palace courtyards directly, there had never been much reason to build the palace defenses any further. And Kartek was glad. Few of the windows even had glass, for this allowed the dry air to waft through the palace to keep it cool. Many of the inner palace walls were only fancy trellises for exactly the same purpose. King Rodrigue of Destin liked to grumble about how this left the palace vulnerable for attack, but Kartek felt the openness allowed the palace to feel far more welcoming to her people than any of the northern castles did. It also allowed her palace to feel like home.

Finally, they reached the seamstress's quarters. Kartek took a deep breath of the oils used to rub the clothing as they entered. She had loved this room as a child, with its neat stacks of fabrics that reached the ceiling, stacked wooden crates of dyes, and baskets of fastidiously organized needles, pins, and threads.

"Good morning, Jahira." Ipy bowed but fixed her sharp eyes on Oni as they walked in. "Oni, I thought I told you to have her here an hour ago."

"That is my fault," Kartek said. "I was healing at the pool this morning. I apologize for the delay. Now, let's begin."

Ipy appeared momentarily mollified, though her satisfaction rarely lasted very long with anyone, least of all Oni. She began directing her assistants to remove Kartek's clothes and put the wedding dress on for its final adjustments.

Kartek really couldn't see why they needed so many adjustments. The green gown seemed nearly as simple as her other dresses, thin so she wouldn't sweat to death in it during the ceremony or after during the feast. Its only real changes from her everyday clothes were the jewels that lined its edges. Pleats ran along the skirt's length, which reached just down to her ankles. Still, the swishing of cool cloth felt good on her skin as they folded and tucked and pinned, and Kartek closed her eyes and tried to picture the day she would actually wear this.

Preparations would begin early in the morning even though the ceremony wouldn't take place until after the sun set. She tried to imagine what it would feel like to have the soft green silk brush her legs as she walked toward Gahiji.

She didn't want to admit it, of course, but Oni had been right when she accused Kartek of being nervous. Not that Kartek didn't trust Gahiji, of course. Her parents had chosen him after looking at dozens of possible suitors. His match was the most obvious for political and military reasons. And though he came from a wild, nomadic people, there was nothing about him to suggest that he might not make a fine husband. Together, Kartek and Gahiji would unite Hedjet and the tribes to create a stronger people in the desert.

But at this very moment, politics were the last thing on Kartek's mind. All she could see in her head was him leaning down to kiss her, a giant of a man who dwarfed even her. And she was considered tall for a woman.

She shuddered.

"Are you well, Jahira?" Ipy paused in her work and looked up at Kartek.

Kartek opened her mouth to assure the woman that she was fine, but a knock sounded at the door. One of the seamstress's girls went to get it. After speaking for a moment with whomever was outside, she returned.

Ipy pulled a pin from her mouth and frowned at the girl. "What is the matter?"

"They say we need to look outside."

If the warble in her voice wasn't enough to put Kartek on edge, the way the girl's face had turned ashen was. Everyone ran to the windows and peered out. When she found her own place at the window, Kartek froze.

To the east, over dunes of glittering sand poured people. Hundreds of people. Like ants they marched forward, turning the dunes from gold to brown, gray, black, and whatever other colors they wore.

"Are they warriors?" one of the girls whispered.

"No," Oni shook her head. "There are women and children among them."

Kartek squinted against the bright reflection of the sand. No colors were carried to denote the tribe's identity. She tried to recall which of the ten tribes had so many people, but none came to mind.

"My jahira."

She turned at the sound of a man's voice. "Ahmos. Which tribe is it?"

Ahmos crossed his arms, the very picture of confidence, but she didn't miss the way he ground his jaw. "Not which tribe, Jahira." He paused and glanced at the women in the room. "It's all of them."

~

To get the rest of The Green-Eyed Prince: A Retelling of The Frog Prince, go to BrittanyFichterFiction.com or Amazon.com. To see the rest of Brittany's collection, continue reading….

~

The Classical Kingdoms Collection

Before Beauty: A Retelling of Beauty and the Beast

Blinding Beauty: A Retelling of The Princess and the Glass Hill

Beauty Beheld: A Retelling of Hansel and Gretel

Girl in the Red Hood: A Retelling of Little Red Riding Hood

Silent Mermaid: A Retelling of The Little Mermaid

Cinders, Stars, and Glass Slippers: A Retelling of Cinderella

Coming soon...

A Curse of Gems: A Retelling of Toads and Diamonds

~

The Classical Kingdoms Collection Novellas

The Green-Eyed Prince: A Retelling of the Frog Prince

~

The Autumn Fair Trilogy

The Autumn Fairy

The Autumn Fairy of Ages

The Last Autumn Fairy

~

The Entwined Tales

1. A Goose Girl: A Retelling of The Goose Girl - KM Shea

2. An Unnatural Beanstalk: A Retelling of Jack and the Beanstalk - Brittany Fichter

3. A Bear's Bride: A Retelling of East of the Sun, West of the Moon - Shari L. Tapscott

4. A Beautiful Curse: A Retelling of The Frog Bride - Kenley Davidson

5. A Little Mermaid: A Retelling of The Little Mermaid - Aya Ling

6. An Inconvenient Princess: A Retelling of Rapunzel - Melanie Cellier

ABOUT THE AUTHOR

Brittany lives with her Prince Charming, their little fairy, and their little prince in a ~~sparkling~~ (decently clean) castle in whatever kingdom the Air Force has most recently placed them. When she's not writing, Brittany can be found enjoying her family (including their spoiled black Labrador), doing chores (she would rather be writing), going to church, belting Disney songs, exercising, or decorating cakes.

Facebook: Facebook.com/BFichterFiction
Subscribe: BrittanyFichterFiction.com
Email: BrittanyFichterFiction@gmail.com
Instagram: @BrittanyFichterFiction
Twitter: @BFichterFiction